A COVID ODYSSEY

SECOND WAVE

A fictional COVID-19 pandemic story

Graham Elder

G.M. Elder Publishing

www.twodocswriting.com
www.grahamelder.com

Printed in Canada and U.S.A.
Cover design by Rebecacovers

ISBN: 978-0-9958907-5-6 (ebook)
ISBN: 978-0-9958907-6-3 (pbk)

To my father, Murray G. Elder, who taught me everything important in life just by being himself.

And to all the healthcare workers around the globe who continue to put their lives on the line daily, battling this disease.

Preface

The information in this novel reflects the scientific thinking and general status of the world leading up to the end of November 2020. This was a pandemic time before vaccines were on the horizon and before there were any real treatment options available. Lockdowns were ongoing, the second wave was looming, and there really wasn't much hope …

Present Day

November 19th, 2020

The blackened night was obliterated by a staccato of lightning bolts that exposed a reality completely at odds with my perfect plan.

How could things have gone so wrong?

To call it rain was far too gentle a word. These were water bullets fired from invisible heights by an angry God. Each solid drop filling our bucket to the point of no return. The wind plastered my hair to the shape of my skull and sucked the terrified breath from my lungs. White knuckles gripped the spokes of the ship's helm and weak, rattling knees fixed a base ready to collapse at any moment. How much more of a beating could the *Rumrunner* take? How much more could *we* take?

A gust crescendoed once more, steamrolling our ship. And then I heard it and felt it. Like an atom had split and the bomb had gone off. A deafening, gigantic, oak-felling crack. I crouched into a semi-fetal position and held fast to the helm.

"Do not let go of this wheel. Under any circumstances," my captain had ordered. I would obey at all costs. I had never been in a war zone, but I was sure it felt very much like this.

Another bolt arced diagonally across the sky and revealed the mainmast broken in two. The top half flailed off the starboard side, partially submerged in thirty-foot swells. The torn, white mainsail dragged like a parachute, pulling the *Rumrunner* over into the suffocating depths of the North Atlantic. We had lowered all of the sails except the reefed main. *We should have dropped the mainsail as well.* With the fuel run dry, we needed forward thrust to steer the ship, to keep from getting broadsided.

Rufus, my captain, emerged from below, with his headlamp glowing a ghostly red, and his fiery Jamaican dreadlocks in complete disarray under a black tuque. But for the lack of an eye patch, he had all the semblance of a crusty, weathered swashbuckler. His face harbored a look of dread. "Mark, *mon*, what the hell was that?"

I stood and stretched an arm, pointing to where the mainmast once lived. "We lost the main. Broken in two with that last gust."

Rufus attempted to shine his light on the area in question, but the night sucked his illumination into oblivion. "Goddammit," he yelled over the howl. "With the sail dragging we're going to get pulled over. We have to cut it loose. We have to cut the stays."

He disappeared for a moment below and quickly reappeared holding a set of bolt cutters. I now understood what we had to do. The top of the mast was secured to the ship's upper deck by long metal cables made up of multiple strands of wires – the stays. Several of them had already snapped, but we had to cut the remaining ones in order to allow the upper half of the mast and sail to disengage from the ship and free us from the hand that was pulling us under.

Rufus yelled, "Come, my friend. You can let go of the wheel. You're not doing anything anymore." He handed me the bolt cutters, and I followed him onto the upper deck where the lower half of the mainmast stood like a rotted, dead tree trunk. As we climbed from the cockpit, gale force winds assaulted us with renewed vigor as the *Rumrunner* bucked and twisted like an untamed bronco. I followed the beam of Rufus' bobbing headlamp, grappling my way across the upper deck. Finally, he pointed to a horizontally directed metal wire that was humming with the pull of the mast and mainsail in the water. "Move over here and cut it," he cried out.

I followed my captain's orders and cut a wire that was the size of my index finger. This was no easy feat, and it felt like I was gnawing through it, one strand at a time. A sheen of sweat soaked my upper back. Eventually, it zinged like a futuristic laser blaster as it released. Rufus' light caught flashes of snakelike whipping motions as the wire disappeared into the ocean. The *Rumrunner* shuddered and seemed to right itself just a little, as if it had found a drop of hope.

"One down, and three to go, my friend," Rufus grinned. We crawled like spiders over the open deck, repeating the same manoeuvres, each cut wire a further blow for freedom. Rufus looked at me, our headlamps shining on each other's faces. "The last one is at the bow and won't be easy. You holding up?"

Frozen fingers on my right hand were curled around one of the handles of the bolt cutter in a death grip. I was shivering from head to toe both from fear and the cold, and the urge to vomit was running a fifty-yard dash up and down my esophagus. Salty sweat melded with ocean spray, torching my eyes. I forced a smile at Rufus and yelled, "Top of the world, Rufus. Top of the world."

We worked our way to the front of the ship, and now, I understood the problem. The center of the ship, where the mainmast is located, is typically the most stable. The bow or front of the ship is the exact opposite. This was the bucking bronco on steroids with a hornet's nest up its ass. The g-forces were off the charts. There was one stay left to cut, and it was attached to the tip of the bowsprit – the eight-foot-long wooden pole at the very front of the ship. To get to it, one of us would have to shimmy along the bowsprit and then somehow hang on, with both hands dedicated to the bolt cutter, fighting the waves, the wind, the rain, and the g-forces. It was a suicide mission.

Rufus said, without discussion, "I'm going, my friend." He tightened the straps on his lifejacket and tied a rope around his waist. He fastened the other end to a nearby cleat and then uncurled my fingers from the bolt cutter.

"Tie yourself off. Hold me in back, by my belt."

A Covid Odyssey Second Wave

I nodded and quickly repeated Rufus' manoeuvre by tying another rope around my waist, securing it to another cleat. Rufus shook his head to clear the water from his eyes and then climbed out and straddled the eight-foot-long bowsprit. Like a kid in a playground, he began shimmying along the pole, an inch at a time, trying to keep his balance as he fought the elements. I kept my hand locked to his belt, climbed out onto the bowsprit, and followed him. I was able to anchor my legs in the netting that hung below the bowsprit. It wasn't much, but it was more than Rufus had where he was. When he reached the tip of the bowsprit, our added weight and the strain of the final stay began to pull the bow under the waves. And then the cycle began, much like an amusement park ride.

One moment, as the *Rumrunner* climbed out of a trough, Rufus and I were sitting high above the water with Rufus working frantically, trying to get the tips of the bolt cutter around the final stay. The next, we were holding our breaths submerged, counting the moments before the *Rumrunner*'s bow would exhale us like a humpback whale's spout, and we could gasp for oxygen once again. This went on and on, interminably. Between the bobs of my headlamp and the arcs of lightning illuminating the sky, I could just make out Rufus' form. Communication was impossible; the turbulence of the gale force winds engulfed all sound. Finally, a wave as tall as a three-story building pulled us deep, and I was sure it was the last ride.

It was strangely calm under the sea. Almost safe, like the anarchic oxygenated world above was another universe, far, far away. The temptation to just let go of the *Rumrunner* and either float up or sink down

– it didn't seem to matter which direction – was overwhelming. And then the g-forces came hard, and my already turbulent stomach sank into my pelvis as the bow exploded out of the water. The beautiful silence was replaced by singing jet engine winds and a deep grumbling thunder. I tried to sweep the salt water out of my eyes with my free hand. *Free hand?* I looked down and realized that in my "free hand" was a belt. Or, rather, the tattered remains of a belt. A loud, unnatural crack broke through the violent sounds around me and drew my attention to the side of the ship. As I turned to look, my peripheral vision caught the image of a cleat attached to shards of wood zinging past my head with a rope fastened to it. *Rufus!*

Another bolt of lightning lit the sky, and I could see that Rufus was gone, no longer straddling the forward end of the bowsprit. The despair wallowing up my spine was cut short as the bow of the *Rumrunner* once again was pulled under the waves by the uncut, forward stay. And then, as the water reached my neck and what little hope I had left vanished, I felt a lurch – the forward stay had finally given way, freeing the ship. The bow righted itself just as the unravelled, cut end of the stay whipped free from the water and lashed across my face. Warmth spread over my cheek. I slowly backed off of the bowsprit. The *Rumrunner* was still bucking but, with the drag of the forward stay gone, the ship was able to handle it.

When both my feet made contact with the deck, I collapsed into a crouched position, untied the safety line around my waist and paused for a moment to catch my breath. *Rufus was gone! One second, he was there, and then ...*

I looked up and heard it more than I saw it. The cut end of the forward stay, still attached to the end of the bowsprit, was whipping haphazardly in the winds. I ducked my head and began to crawl back to the cockpit. And then I felt the scorching sting as the flailing wire attacked me once more, this time slicing open my shoulder.

I shouted to the sky, "Fuuuuuuck! C'mon, just one single break!"

Unlike my frozen face, I could feel the shoulder. A sharp, searing pain radiated down my arm. Miraculously, my headlamp was still functioning, and I could see thin rivers of blood flowing down the yellow sleeve of my rain jacket. And just beyond the edge of the light, between me and the safety of the cockpit, the long flapping end of the stay lay in wait, carving up the night randomly, blocking my path.

For a moment, I stood hypnotized, watching the gleam of the flagellating wire. It's thin, silver-coloured body careened off the remnants of the mainmast and zig-zagged through the dark, high over my head. I was reminded of drawing names in the night sky with sparklers as a kid at camp. It suddenly dawned on me that this tail end of the stay was still attached to the front of the bowsprit and must be twenty or thirty feet long. At that length, Rufus must have severed it *after* he had been thrown from the *Rumrunner, while* he was underwater. The captain who would do anything to save his ship and his crew.

I took a deep breath. If Rufus was willing to give his life to save mine, the least I could do was survive. I stood up, a new surge of adrenaline fueling my legs. I closed my eyes hard to squeeze away the saltwater and improve my night vision. When I opened them, it was like the lumens of my flashlight had tripled in power. I zeroed in on the metallic glint that was the unraveled tip of the stay thrashing high overhead. Once I had a lock on it, I advanced with my good arm outstretched in front, ready to fend off this deadly "weapon" given life by the storm.

Suddenly, as if it sensed my desperation, it arced downwards, like a great leviathan, and attacked. First time – my thigh. Second time – my chest. Stinging instead of cutting, as if trifling with me, testing me. And then it struck fast and hard, going for the kill. It was like looking down the end of a gun barrel as a bullet emerged, targeting my forehead. My head reflexively dodged to one side as my good arm grabbed the head of the cobra and held on for dear life. It pulled and snapped. Pushed and kicked. Finally, a brief lull in the wind allowed me to tie it off to a nearby safety rail. I paused for a moment to examine the tip of the now still wire, which had completely unravelled. Bits of bloodied, shredded skin were enmeshed in its entanglement. *My* skin. *My* blood. *My God!*

***

I sat at the kitchen table in the main cabin with my feet immersed in a foot of ice-cold ocean water. As suddenly as the storm had come on, like Rufus, it was gone. But the *Rumrunner* was still sinking. Slowly, but surely. Built in 1912, its wooden hull could not stand up to the hours of incessant battering that the storm had delivered. Particularly since we had struck some errant object floating aimlessly the night before which had left a hole the size of a small cannonball in the hull on the starboard bow below the water line. Initially, it was manageable. Over time, with the pounding of the waves, the hole expanded, and we didn't have the skill or the materials to plug it. We had no fuel, which meant no power. No power meant no bilge pumps. There was no way around this: the *Rumrunner* would be lost to the Atlantic Ocean.

Plan B was the Beaufort life raft. Unfortunately, it was among the casualties of the storm and had gone over the side at some point during our cutting-the-stays expedition. Plan C? There was no plan C. *Abandon ship and swim?*

"Ha," I laughed out loud to myself. At best, I was an average swimmer. But I *was* a good floater. "Ha," I laughed again, the sound of my voice echoing faintly around the empty cabin, dampened by the rising water level. It was deathly quiet now that the storm had settled. The engines were still, and the ship was drifting on the currents. The cabin was illuminated by three green glow sticks I had found in an emergency kit. "Eerie" didn't begin to describe the scene.

I had tried to cross the Atlantic Ocean in search of the 2020 version of the holy grail ... *and failed.* I'd left behind my beautiful wife and –

"Shit!"

I grabbed for a handhold as the *Rumrunner* abruptly shuddered and lurched. An air pocket dislodged, sounding like a heavy belch. The *Rumrunner* then stabilized once more, but now, it felt even more like a ticking nuclear timebomb waiting to implode. I released the handhold and sighed nervously. The "belch" had reminded me of poker nights with the boys and my Golden Retriever, Archie, laying at my feet. All of sudden, I felt miserably homesick. My spiraling despair, however, was overshadowed by the pain in my cheek and shoulder, which was worsening now that my adrenaline was spent.

I looked up and spotted the door to the liquor cabinet swinging freely, the faintest squeak audible from the old brass hinges. Definitely a sign. I needed liquid courage and some general antiseptic. I reached in deep to the back – Rufus always kept the good stuff buried deep – and pulled out a bottle of rum and a bottle of vodka. I squinted in the glow to make out the label on the rum. This wasn't just any rum; this was a limited edition Mount Gay Tricentennial Selection that Rufus had mentioned. The one he was saving for a special occasion. The one he never got a chance to taste. Well, abandoning a ship named the *Rumrunner* to Davey Jones' locker struck me as a special *rum*-worthy occasion. Or, at least, an appropriate one. I cracked the plastic around the bottle neck and gently removed the cork. For a second, I thought about getting a glass.

"Fuck it."

I lifted the bottle to my lips and poured it down my hatch. The burning notes of oak, caramel and vanilla flooded my senses and seemed to course everywhere in my body at once. I released a long sigh and smiled for the first time in many hours.

Using the mirror in the head and a small flashlight propped up on the sink – my headlamp had finally died – I was able to clean out the wound on my face and sterilize it with very expensive vodka. I found sterile glue, Steri-Strips, and bandages in the first aid kit and applied them. If I was going swimming, the last thing I needed was to leave a trail of blood for the sharks to follow. I then did the same with my shoulder. Fortunately, neither wound seem to require stitches. Or, at least, I had staunched the bleeding and could get by for now without them.

I took another long pull from the rum bottle and then it hit me hard, like a sledge coming down on an anvil. *I'm going to die*. Maybe today. Whatever day today was. The water level inside the boat was now at knee level. An N95 mask floated past me in the cabin. I picked it out of the water and stared at it, thinking back to the significance it had taken on since the first wave of Covid had descended upon the earth. Protection *for* me, protection *from* me, fashion statement, a statement of individuality. Like all that really mattered for me, now.

A buzzing sound vibrated against my chest. I thought I was having a cardiac arrhythmia until I realized I had tucked my cell phone inside the breast pocket of my weather jacket when the storm worsened. *Why would it be ringing? We were way outside cell phone range. Weren't we?*

I reached in and pulled out my phone, expecting … what? Maybe Sarah? There was no caller ID.

"Hello. Is anyone there?" I asked.

"Of course, there's someone here. What would be the point of calling if I wasn't here?"

It took me a long moment to recognize a voice I hadn't heard in many months. "Hitchhiker?"

"Sarah contacted me via email," the voice continued. "Presumably, from your laptop. You know, you really shouldn't allow others access to your password. Even your wife."

"What … how are you –"

"She's terribly worried. Said you'd left two weeks ago on some ridiculous quest to find a cure for Covid. Your learning curve seems incredibly steep. Is this about that file you sent me from your father?"

"Maybe. Yes," I replied.

"Hmm, well, to tell you the truth – and I hate agreeing with you – he might be on to something. Still, are you really trying to cross the Atlantic Ocean on a pleasure yacht in November?"

"There was no other –"

"You really love the adventure, don't you? Or maybe the adventure just loves you?"

My mind was reeling. I was on a sinking ship being chastised by my new American friend – who, I'm sure, was sitting quite comfortably in a very dry living room in the warmth of his home. We had had intermittent contact via email since my ordeal this past March when, in a roundabout way, he had helped save my wife after I picked him up hitchhiking through Kentucky on my way to Florida during the early stages of the Covid lockdown. He never did tell me his name.

"Fuck off, Hitchhiker. I was just trying to save the world, and now, I'm stuck on a sinking ship in the middle of the ocean."

"Why don't you just call for help?"

"Well, the cell phone wasn't working until you –"

"And you can't be in the middle of the ocean if you're receiving a cell call. You must be close enough to shore to pick up the land-based cell towers."

"I …" He was right. During the storm, we must have drifted a lot further east than I thought.

"In fact, as much as you know I hate smartphones, this may be that one occasion where it could save your life. Hit that Google Maps app. Like that one you were using in the pickup truck when we first met. Plus, you must have some charts handy. See if you can cross reference your location on Google Maps to the chart. See exactly where you are."

"Right. Right. Thanks, Hitchhiker, that might work."

I looked at my phone and noted only 20% battery life left. My lousy phone had a propensity to suddenly die with no warning. I had to work fast. In fact, better than his idea, I had a marine navigation app that I'd forgotten about since it required cell phone towers to work and there weren't many of those in the middle of the ocean. I activated the app and waited. My reception was hovering between one and two bars.

"Listen … Hitchhiker, I appreciate your help. I may only have a few minutes of battery power left –"

"Typical smartphones, if they're not sucking your mind dry, they're continuously disappointing –"

"HITCHHIKER!! Listen, I don't have much time. Can you do something for me? Can you tell Sarah I love her, and I miss her, and …" Tears were welling up and my heart was aching almost as much as the rest of my storm-battered body.

"And you wish you'd never left."

"No! No, that's not true. I had to do it. If there's even a chance of a cure …"

"I'll relay the message. So … where are you?"

I had almost forgotten. Five percent battery remaining. I looked at the map, and there it was. Or rather, there *I* was. The *Rumrunner* was just outside the shipping channels of Southampton and drifting towards them. Maybe … I had a chance. If I could just get into the channels.

One percent battery left. A large bubble dislodged from somewhere in the bowels of the ship and then the *Rumrunner* began to tilt forward, like a submarine diving.

"Hitchhiker, my phone's running dry. I'm just outside of the channels heading into Southampton. I'll have to swim for it. Tell Sarah I love her …"

The screen went blank.

I sat for a moment, collecting my thoughts and my regrets. I placed my phone back inside the breast pocket of my weather jacket, for all the good it would do now. I stared emptily into a cubby hole above the table and noticed Rufus' wallet resting next to his satellite phone. Without thinking, I grabbed the wallet and stuffed it into a pocket.

I then picked up the satellite phone and clicked the 'on' switch. Nothing. It had never worked properly from day one of the trip, and now its battery was as dead as any delusions I had of surviving this journey. I sighed and tossed the phone into water that was now waist high. I no longer had any chance of communication with the outside world.

I groaned heavily as I stood with joints stiffened by the cold and the humidity. I zipped up my weather jacket, secured my life vest and then donned a second, larger life vest over my first. If one was good surely two would be better. I grabbed two bottles of water and stuffed them inside my jacket. I clipped my black backpack to one of the straps on my life vest. There wasn't much more than clothes in it, but it had seen me through many adventures and had become somewhat of a lucky charm. Finally, I donned a wool tuque and a pair of thick leather gloves and then waded through waist deep water up the ladder and into the cockpit.

It was still pitch black outside, but at least now there were stars. I could just make out Cassiopeia and the North Star. The clouds from the storm had moved to wreak havoc somewhere else, and the water was mirror calm. I climbed up on the transom and sat. Waiting. The bow was now completely submerged. It was time to leave. I didn't want to get caught up in lines that were still floating freely. Lines that could knot themselves and drag me under.

The water remained brutally cold yet, somehow, I was acclimatizing. I sat there, frozen in time and space. I didn't want to leave but, clearly, I couldn't stay. As the water crested my shoulders and enveloped me like mother nature's womb, I pushed off, floating away from the *Rumrunner* and into the starry night. I looked back and could see only darkness. And then I heard it: large lava like bubble sounds as the *Rumrunner* was swallowed by the sea. I was completely alone.

How the hell did I get here?

18 Days Earlier

November 1st, 2020

"A flying cat?"

"Yeah."

"He thought he was a flying cat and then jumped from a fourth story window?"

"Yup, meth will do that to you."

"He *does* know that cats don't fly."

"He does *now*."

A morose cackle broke out on the other end of the line. "You guys down in the emergency room are sick puppies. I love it. Listen, I'm just going into a two-hour case. What's the damage?"

I was on the phone with Rick, the orthopedic surgeon on call. "Stable lumbar spine fracture, undisplaced pelvis fracture, ankle fractures on both sides that are bad, right wrist scaphoid fracture that's undisplaced, left wrist distal radius fracture which is quite angulated and a broken jaw. Other than that, he seems a like a healthy, decent guy."

"Yeah, right," Rick snarled. "Meth, and what else?"

"The usual: coke, opiates, and cannabis. At least that's what he admits to. Urine tox screen is still pending."

"Damn addicts. They're frustrating as hell. It feels like they eat up more of our tax dollars than the rest of the medical system combined."

I paused for a moment before I pushed against the medical grain. "Rick, he's just a guy who's taken a bad life turn. Could happen to any of us."

"Mark? You haven't gone soft from extended vacation time, have you?"

"Hey, I'm just saying …"

"Alright, alright, let's see how long this conscientious, new and improved *you* lasts down there. Get a head to toe CT scan. Splint both ankles and the right wrist. Have a go at reducing the left wrist, and I'll be down after my case is finished."

"All done and I was just about to reduce his wrist."

"Damn, it's good to have you back, Mark. The administration may not have missed you, but we sure did. We should grab a beer sometime. Y'know, Covid permitting."

"Yeah, I know. It's good to *be* back. I was going nuts sitting at home for eight months."

"Well, I suppose it could have been worse. Listen, my patient's asleep under GA. Gotta go. Talk to you – Wait. He's Cov Neg?"

"Likely, but don't worry. Rapid test will be done by the time he's ready for the OR."

"Great. It's a killer doing these cases with full Covid PPE over lead aprons."

"Roger that. Don't worry, one day we'll have a vaccine."

"Yeah, one day."

I hung up the phone. Rick was right about my forced leave of absence; it could have been a lot worse – like criminal charges and jail time worse. I had gotten off light, but I'd still been away from my job for eight months and felt rusty as hell. I inhaled deeply, straightened my spine, adjusted my mask and face shield, and then went back to the trauma bay. I looked at the attending nurse and asked, "Everything okay?"

"All good," she replied. "What did ortho say?"

"The usual, 'Busy right now. Patch 'em up. Be down later.'"

"I'll call the respiratory tech back so we can deal with the wrist?"

"Sounds like a plan. Can you draw up some Fentanyl and Versed?"

"Sure. You know, a lot of the guys are using Propafol now."

"Right, Milk of Amnesia. It's okay. I'll stick with what I know. For now."

Eight months away and it's a whole new world.

"No problem." As she left the trauma bay for the medication room, she looked back at me and, with smiling eyes, said, "It's good to have you back, Mark."

I smiled under my mask, gave her a thank you nod, and then busied myself preparing the patient for the procedure on his wrist. I dug through the cast cart and found finger traps – like the Chinese finger trap toys – and then placed one on his index and one on his middle finger. I passed a small rope through the clasps and then up around the boom of the trauma bay surgical lights. I tugged the rope tight until the deformed wrist was hanging straight in the air. The flying cat jumper didn't budge. I wondered if I'd really need any medications to sedate him, he was pretty snowed from his recreational anesthetic already. Both the nurse and respiratory tech returned at the same time.

"Hey, Mark," the respiratory tech said, taking his position at the head of the bed and adjusting the monitors, "I just ran into Sarah. She says she's been texting you all morning, but you haven't responded. She says she's too busy to get away from the pharmacy. Can you head over when you're done? She's got an important message for you."

"Will do. I dropped my phone getting out of the car in the parking lot this morning and then somehow managed to step on it."

"Ouch. Terminal event?"

"Hopefully, just a cracked screen."

"I feel for you, man. I broke my phone, once. Felt like I'd lost my best friend." Tony was 27 years old and lived a second life on his phone. Literally, he was involved in a game where he logged six to eight hours a day as an avatar. For him, losing his phone would be like losing his other self.

"Okay, now that everyone's here, please give Mr. Flying Cat the Versed and Fentanyl cocktail. Let's see if we can't impress the orthopaedic team and make this wrist ana-fucking-tomic!"

***

It was 3 PM and my eight-hour shift was over. My feet weighed heavy as I trudged down the hallway with my pack slung over my shoulder. I'd forgotten what a busy eight-hour shift in the ER could do to a person. I was physically drained and mentally decision depleted. One more decision and I would probably toss up my slice of welcome back lunch pizza. I still hadn't spoken to Sarah; we'd played phone tag all day. Now that my mind had left all the medical stuff in the ER – or at least as much as you ever could – I was left with some room to wonder about Sarah's message. What could be so important? Was someone sick? A relative? A friend? Archie? I arrived at the pharmacy and flashed my ID at the door entry scanner. Big, blinking, red-light zero. Apparently, I'd also forgotten that my access privileges had been revoked while I was on probation. This would take some getting used to. I pressed the doorbell and a few seconds later Sarah stood before me.

"Hey, you." Sarah said, her brow furrowed. "I was just heading to the ER. Why didn't you just come in?"

I looked pointedly at the security scanner and tilted my head.

"Yeah, right. Sorry, I forgot. It's only for six months, Mark."

"I know," I replied, "but it's a bit of a downer to go from chief of the department with trusted access to almost everywhere in the hospital to … this." I held up my new ID badge which, in small lettering under my name, said words like "probation" and "limited access."

Sarah gave me a forlorn smile, clasped her arms around my waist and pulled me in.

I whispered into her ear, "You know, we're not supposed to have any physical contact at work. Part of my probation. Your presence could affect my judgement and all that."

She whispered back, "Screw 'em. You're my husband and the father of our new baby. By the laws of Sarah, we can hug whenever we want."

I pushed her back just far enough to make eye contact. "Wait." I stammered, "The father of what?"

"Our new baby. The test was positive. I was going to surprise you at dinner, but … you really looked like you needed some good news."

"We're going to have a baby? I can't believe it … a baby … a new baby …"

I really couldn't think of anything intelligent to say, so I just hugged her harder and buried my face in her neck as a joyful tear trickled down under my mask. The pharmacy door opened, and someone said, "Get a room you two. Oh, and congrats, Mark. You'll make a wonderful father. And welcome back. You're my hero, brother-in-law. You're everyone's hero." Jenna, Sarah's sister and pharmacist co-worker, squeezed my shoulder and then headed down the hall. She called back, "See you this weekend for dinner. I might invite a new friend, just to push the bubble."

"Jenna is seeing someone?" I asked, taking Sarah's hand, and leading her down a different corridor to the parking lot.

"Apparently, but she won't divulge who. It's someone at the hospital. A surgeon, I think."

"Geez, it better not be Rick. That guy's a blast, but he's not known for monogamy."

"Guess we'll find out at –" Sarah suddenly stood statue still. "Shit. Mark, there's something else. It's why I've been trying to reach you all day."

"Something else besides the fact that we're pregnant?"

"Yes, your mother left a message on my phone."

"My mum? Called from England? Why?"

"It's your dad, Mark, he's not doing well."

***

Sarah and I pulled into our driveway at the same time after a short, ten-minute, traffic-free drive – the benefits of living in a smallish town in Northern Ontario. Even though our shifts were finishing at the same time today, we had taken separate vehicles. While Sarah's workday had a predictable endpoint, mine frequently ran over.

My thoughts were in a continuous tug of war loop during the drive home. Yahoo, we're finally pregnant! – Shit! Dad's not doing well. I assumed it was the dementia worsening. Had he wandered off again and hurt himself?

"Any luck?" I asked, my head peering over the top of my Highlander as I shut the car door. Since my phone was out of commission, I'd asked Sarah to try contacting my mother, telling her I'd call as soon as we got home.

"No. I left two messages, though. I'm sure she'll call back soon." I noticed Sarah was carrying a second, much heavier briefcase, in addition to her own, as she made her way to the front door.

"Whoa. Hold on there. Let me grab that for you." I reached for the heavy briefcase, which she gave up readily.

"Am I to enjoy this level of chivalry for the entire pregnancy?" she asked.

"At least for the first trimester," I responded, grinning as I grabbed for her hand to help her up the stairs. "It *is* the most vulnerable period."

"That's quite alright, Sir Lance-a-Little. Save it for when I've got cankles and a trucker's belly."

I laughed. "What's with this behemoth," I asked, raising the briefcase a few millimeters.

"New work protocols. With the second wave beginning, we're going to an alternate day, work-from-home schedule." It was her turn to grin as she said this.

"I can see you're greatly distressed by this news."

"Oh yeah, Mister. My turn to prance around in my pyjamas all day. Or, at least, pyjama bottoms. Looks like there'll be a few Zoom meetings to attend."

"Well, you'll see. That schtick loses its appeal very quickly." I unlocked and opened the front door, and we were quickly greeted by our furry, four-legged first child, Archie. He stood on his hind legs and pawed both of us simultaneously.

"Down, Archie." I dropped to one knee, letting my backpack and briefcase fall to the floor. I let him lick my face as I brushed golden red hair out of his eyes. "Looks like someone needs a haircut."

"Bonus with you at home more," I continued. "Archie will have some company, again."

A ringing sound came from the kitchen. I ran for the phone and picked it up. A call on the landline was either my mother or some automated scam.

"Hello? Mum?"

"Mark? I've been trying to reach you all day."

"Sorry. I was at work, and my cell broke this morning. What's going on? What's this about dad?" I could feel my heart rate accelerating, and it wasn't from my five-yard sprint to answer the phone.

"Mark, your dad began feeling ill a few days ago. He was taken by ambulance to UHS this morning when he couldn't catch his breath anymore. *He tested positive for Covid ...*"

This last statement was left hanging, full of angst and different meanings for different people. For older, it could be the kiss of death. For younger, a two-week paid vacation from work to increase their rankings on Call of Duty. For someone like me, in my early forties, it could be as bad as weeks of wanting to die. When I had COVID-19 in March, after coming back from Florida and a failed mission to save my wife, I was in the "wanting to die" category. I had never felt sicker in my life. It was as if I'd been sent to hell for a couple of weeks to teach me a lesson for all the idiocy I exhibited trying to get to Sarah.

"Mum, Dad may be in his eighties, but he's healthy and strong and –"

"Mark, he's not doing well. He's on oxygen and several new medications. They're debating whether or not he's a candidate for a ventilator."

A Covid Odyssey Second Wave

My knees buckled, and I had to grasp the counter to stabilize my world. I reached for breath that would not come. I could feel Sarah at my side, her hand on my elbow. My mother had a matter-of-fact way of delivering bad news. Likely, from years of living with a microbiologist whose entire world consisted of beings that exist only at the microscopic level. My dad had been one of the top virologists in Britain, and the epitome of a scientist. His lab coat was his persona, and he wore thick glasses as if it would allow him to see his study subjects more clearly. Now he was experiencing his work from the other side of the fence.

"Mum, I'm really sor –"

"I know, Mark. I am too. I'm not calling to commiserate. I know you and your father haven't gotten along over the past many years. Your dad has had a great life. Exactly the life he wanted. Not everyone gets that. As you said, he's strong and generally healthy, so I think he's got a fighting chance."

"How are you feeling … physically, Mum?" I asked.

"My Covid test was negative. I'm in quarantine at home right now for another –" She paused here, and I could hear her whispering to herself, "– another eleven days. I feel fine, actually. To be honest, your father and I haven't been together very much for the past eight months. Since Covid made its appearance, he's been down in his basement – his cave – doing research and, I think, running experiments. Which brings me to my other point: there are two envelopes."

"Two envelopes?"

"Yes. From your father. One, I posted to you this morning. The other is waiting for you here."

My head was spinning with questions, but, for some reason, I latched on to a stupid, unimportant one. "Okay, why not mail both of them to me at the same time, in the same envelope?"

"It's what he wanted. I don't know why."

I tried to access my logical mind, to figure out what my dad could have been thinking. A will? My parents were reasonably well off, but certainly nothing that would command this kind of urgency. "Alright, I can expect the first envelope in a couple of days, I guess. Courier?"

"Yes, of course. He said it was something to convince you."

"Convince me? Convince me of what?" *To go to England? Help my mother if Dad dies?*

"Again. I really don't know."

"Okay, but you have the second envelope. Right?"

"He left it for you in the basement."

"Perfect. Then just go get it, open it, and see what it says."

My mother took a loud, weighted breath that reminded me of her picking up a new story book when I was a young child – just before she read the first words. She once said that she didn't want to run out of breath and ruin the momentum of the story. "Mark, your dad has been working in his lab day and night since the cases in Wuhan were announced to the world last November. At first, there were people coming at all hours of the day, pushing dollies filled with boxes of every size. Some of the people I recognized as former colleagues from his work at Porton Down. His dementia was worsening with more frequent memory lapses, and I thought his friends were just appeasing him for old time's sake. I now suspect it was something more than that. I'm not exactly sure what he was doing down there, but it definitely involved the coronavirus outbreak. I'm assuming the envelopes have something to do with that. Before the ambulance came and brought him to the hospital, he made me swear that I mail one envelope to you. The other, he said, 'would be waiting for you in the basement.' He also made me promise not to go down there, to leave everything as is until you arrived."

"Right. Okay, Mum. The envelope's waiting for me in the basement. You just said, 'Dad wasn't in his right mind,' especially with the Covid infection. Forget what he said and just go to the basement, get the envelope, open it, and read it to me."

"Mark, I'm not an idiotic, devoted, fifty's housewife from an old sitcom. Of course, I've been down to the basement. Do you think even for a second I would listen to your father? He's a silly old fool and I love him dearly, but it's clear his mind hasn't been working as well as it once did."

"So. Why can't –?"

"– It's in a safe, Mark. A very large and heavy safe that Porton Down cemented into our foundation many years ago. At the height of his career, your father was working with highly classified military information. It can only be opened by a thumbprint scan. Your father said the second envelope was inside the safe and only you could access it."

My frustration was building a head of steam. What the hell could be so important that only I could see it, and that it would be locked in a high-grade military safe? Once again, I locked onto a relatively stupid and unimportant question.

"How the hell would he even have my fingerprints?"

I haven't seen him in over a decade.

"I have no idea, Mark. But now you understand why only you can access the envelope. In any case, he was adamant that it would only mean something to you if you read it in his lab."

"Mean what to me? Dad's been retired for years with progressive cognitive decline. What could he possibly have stumbled upon in his basement that was so important?"

"He was very confused before the ambulance came, in and out of consciousness. I really don't know if you can believe anything he was saying but, during one if his more lucid moments, he told me that he had discovered it."

"Discovered what?"

"A cure, Mark. A cure for COVID-19."

***

I remember ...

"Mum, shouldn't we wait for Dad?" I ran into the kitchen from our backyard, where a dozen friends were gathered to celebrate my seventh birthday. It was Saturday afternoon, and everyone was starting to converge around the picnic table. They knew the cake would be coming soon. I didn't see my father anywhere.

"Mark, your dad just called. He can't make it. He's busy at his new work."

"But Mum. Dad always watches me blow out my candles. He takes the photograph. We can wait a bit more."

My mother placed one hand on each of my shoulders and stooped over to look me square in the eye. "He said he's very sorry and to go on without him. He won't be home until very late. He did leave a special present for you."

My mother reached into a bag on the counter and produced a rectangular package wrapped in off-white paper decorated with dinosaurs and a large red bow. She placed it in my outstretched hands. The gift tag read, "To Mark, from Dad. Happy 7th Birthday."

I stared at it for a long moment and then gave the package back to my mother. "It's no problem, Mum, he can give it to me tomorrow." I turned and ran back outside.

Every morning for three days my mother tried to give me the present, my dad having either already left for work or, as often as not, having never come home. I refused every day. Finally, on the fourth day, my mother said, "Mark, your father has been very busy and wants you to open the present today. It's something very special he wants you to build for him."

My curiosity overcame my stubbornness, and I tore open the package.

I was six years old when my dad started working at Porton Down. It was like I never saw him again.

17 Days Earlier

November 2nd, 2020

"Still looking?"

A distant female voice asked from somewhere behind me.

I was standing in front of our large bay windows overlooking St. Mary's River with binoculars glued to my face watching two large, ghostly freighters pass each other in the shipping lanes. First sun twinkled off the windows of both their wheelhouses as they cut through the early morning fog that blanketed the uncharacteristically flat waters. Memories of eight months earlier swirled through my mind and superimposed themselves on the scene playing out before me.

"I stiiiiilllll haven't foooooound what I'm looking for," I sang in a croaky voice. Sarah was referring to my red kayak that I'd abandoned trying to cross St. Mary's during my "rescue mission."

"Ahh, some semblance of U2 to start the day …, if Bono were Kermit the Frog."

"I probably sound better in the shower at this hour."

Well, regarding your kayak, while I admire your hopefulness, I think it's time you started looking for another." I felt the warmth of her body, housecoat and all, enclose me from behind.

"You're probably right, but no harm in looking." There was really no chance of my kayak being found anywhere close to here since the currents of the river would have dragged it far downstream. Still, every morning I scanned the waters, hoping.

"What were you thinking, my husband?"

"Thinking? I was only thinking about you at the time. About getting to you and getting you home safe."

She squeezed my waist harder. "Silly man. I meant, 'What were you thinking' *right now*, standing here staring out at the break of dawn, hours before you have to go to work?"

"Ahh. Well, I couldn't sleep. I was thinking about all the reasons preventing me from going to see my mum and dad."

I turned to face her, and we both opened our housecoats, snuggling our bodies together, fighting off the feelings of a coming winter. "Did I wake you?" I asked.

"Not really. I'm afraid my stomach did. A little first trimester nausea and vomiting to start the day."

"Sorry to hear that. You do look a little ashen with a touch of green around the edges."

"Thanks. That's what every pregnant wife wants to hear first thing in the morning."

"Better now?"

"Yes, all better." Sarah tucked her head into my shoulder and there was a long pause before she asked, "You're not *really* thinking of going, are you, Mark?"

This question had been weighing heavily upon my soul since I'd hung up the phone last evening. "Of course not. There are a million reasons why it would be insane."

"Such as?"

"It's my first week back at work and we're short staffed because every time someone gets a headache or a runny nose they're benched until their Covid test comes back or their quarantine period is over. Not to mention, I'm on probation for six months, and I have to pull more than my weight to regain trust and get back to ground zero."

"Very true."

"And, as the second wave ramps up, the world is a crazy place out there with travel rules changing faster than you can say, *Jet Aiiiiiiirliiiiiiner.*"

"Hmm, another musical reference. Steve Miller Band?"

"You got it."

Sarah rolled her eyes at me. "That's it? Just the two reasons? The future of your career as an ER doc and the Covid pandemic landscape?"

I scratched the stubble on my chin. "There's the danger and very real possibility of catching Covid again during any travels."

"Wait, since you've already had it, wouldn't you be immune?"

"If it's a first wave virus, my antibody protection might have waned. Alternatively, if this is a *real* second wave with a newly mutated virus, I could definitely catch it, again. In both cases, it would probably be milder, but –"

"– But you don't know that for sure," Sarah continued. "It could be another full-blown case that puts you in the ICU in some foreign, overcrowded hospital where you don't know anyone."

"True," I said.

"So, that's three solid, concrete, inarguable reasons why you shouldn't go." Sarah was obviously building her wall one stone at a time. It was time for a rebuttal.

"On the other hand, my father, who is a completely self-absorbed workaholic asshole, has Covid and might be dying. My mother obviously would benefit from some support. Although she's always been very self-reliant and independent."

"Exactly, she's super self-reliant. She doesn't really need you."

"Of course, there's the idea that my half-demented father – once upon a time, a brilliant mind and highly published virologist – actually has discovered some kind of cure."

"And the chances of that are …?"

"Pretty much zero, since the last time my mother and I spoke about him, he apparently had forgotten my name, your name, and that particular day had his pants on backwards."

Sarah pushed away just a little, enough to look me in the eye. "And there's no other reason why you shouldn't go to England?"

I reached out and smudged a little dried sleep crust from the corner of her eye. "I suppose after five years of IVF, a pregnant wife might be a good reason."

"You suppose? There was a pause as a sly look came over Sarah's face. She wiggled her pelvis suggestively and whispered, "Hey, Romeo, what's going on down there?"

I smiled and leaned in for a long, hard kiss.

16 Days Earlier

November 3rd, 2020

I dragged my weary ass up the stairs to my front door, each step a small mountain to climb. At the end of my day shift, Phil, my relief, had called in with a sore throat. There was no one else to cover, and so I did a double shift.

Of course, it couldn't have been busier: a drugged out, barefoot, forty-going-on-sixty-year-old female, with a needle still lodged in a vein between her first and second toes and another sticking out of a vein in her temple, had passed out on a side road and then been run over by an SUV. All the bones on her right side were broken, with many of them poking through the skin, in addition to a perforated colon and a ruptured spleen. It was a miracle she made it to the operating room. The icing on the cake was the poor fellow (a 38-year-old father of two young girls) who unwittingly ran her over. When he stepped out of his vehicle and saw the carnage, he immediately had an MI. He was, unfortunately, genetically predisposed to cardiac disease with a strong family history that included two brothers who'd passed away in their forties. Despite two hours of resuscitation efforts, his heart refused to reanimate.

And then there were the three ladies in their late eighties from the same nursing home who somehow stroked out at almost the exact same time. Involving the same side, no less. I strongly advised another woman from the same home (in for a urinary tract infection) not to drink the water there. Not to mention the three broken wrists, four lacerations, two hip fractures … and on and on. At the end of my second shift, my two horrendous weeks with Covid was looking like a vacation.

I opened the front door to the beep-beep sound of our alarm, dumped my backpack on the floor, and then made my way into the kitchen in dire need of sustenance, anything would do. I found Sarah sitting at the island counter nursing a cup of tea and some crackers. Archie was at her feet, sound asleep – not much of a guard dog. A brown envelope lay in front of her with an open Purolator packaging next to it.

"You look exhausted, Mark," she said.

"The second shift was a total train wreck," I replied, opening the door to the fridge, my eye still on the envelope. "Our poor little northern town was hemorrhaging absolute misery this evening from every walk of life."

"Sounds like karmic payback for your time off."

"That's what I was thinking. Or just bad luck."

"For you or your patients?"

"Both, I guess."

"Still a lot of addiction issues?"

"Constantly. I had to jam one very high-strung patient behind a door to prevent her from taking a swing at me while I was waiting for security. She kept spitting over the top of the door trying to nail me. It's hard not to hate them." The light in the fridge suddenly flickered and died. I stood numbly in place, not sure what to do. I sighed. "There's a sad undercurrent in this town right now."

"Just remember, Mark, they're real people with real disease."

"Is that the healthcare professional in you talking?"

"No. That's the little angel on your shoulder called your wife, trying to keep you on the straight and narrow."

"And I love you for it." I spread my hands towards the frustratingly darkened fridge and gave her a spent smile. "Hey, any leftovers?"

"I left a plate of lasagna for you in the oven."

"Excellent. I'm as famished as I am tired." I closed the fridge door, grabbed an oven mitt, and transferred the steaming plate of lasagna to a place setting in front of Sarah, *and the envelope.*

"So?" I asked, eyeing the envelope.

Sarah's face became unreadable. It wasn't a blank look, it was more of a look that, in all the years we'd been together, I'd never seen before and couldn't make out. "I haven't opened it. It's from your dad and addressed to you specifically. In his hand scrawl. It didn't feel right."

I stared at the brown 8 x 11 ½ inch envelope. I was certainly curious, but I couldn't suppress the sense of foreboding and angst that was emanating from it. As if it might contain a life altering secret that would lure me into darkened waters – a siren's song …. I looked at Sarah and could now understand. She was afraid, and she was trying to hide it.

I clanked my fork down, and said, "Shit. Okay. Let's see how the old man planned to convince me." I carefully ripped open the envelope. Inside was a single sheet of yellow paper that I held up to the light and read.

"God damn him."

***

I remember ...

"Mum, look. I finished it." I stood in the kitchen, bare feet firmly planted in front of my mother, supporting a large second world war Spitfire model airplane with both hands. It was by far the largest and most complex model I had ever built, and it took me almost a week of my after-school life. I was standing tall with a gleam in my eyes. "Do you think dad will like it?"

"Honey, it's perfect. I'm sure he'll love it."

Unexpectedly, the front door opened, and I heard the heavy footsteps of my father approach. I ran to the hallway. My dad was carrying one large brief case in each hand and still had his hat and overcoat on.

It must have been raining outside, because I could see wet outlines of his footprints on the oak floors of the hallway.

I came to a sudden stop a few feet in front of him with my chest puffed out and the model airplane in my outstretched hands, as if it were the Queen's diamond crown. "Dad, Dad. Look. I did it. I finished it."

He stared down at me from a mile high, frowned and then mumbled, "Not now, Mark. I've made a breakthrough."

He then shouted towards the kitchen as he pushed the door to the basement open and descended the stairs. "Frances, I'll take my dinner in the basement."

The door closed behind him with a hurtful click.

13 Days Earlier

November 6th, 2020

"You've got your passport? Wallet? Phone? Some cash?"

"Yes, to all …. Wait, my phone!" I frantically patted down my jacket pockets. Sarah touched on the brakes for just a second as we pulled out of the driveway. "Check the outside pocket of your backpack."

"Yup, okay, good. Got it," I replied. "I've got everything."

"Your phone's fully fixed and charged?" Sarah already knew I'd brought my phone in yesterday and had it repaired. She sounded more nervous than I was.

"Yes, ma'am. Fully charged and fixed." We were driving along Queen Street. It was a twenty-minute drive to the airport. Raindrops sprinkled the windshield and the wind had picked up.

"Looks like the weather's turning," Sarah stated. "Maybe your flight won't leave."

"Well, today's flight was the only one with available seating leaving for England from Montreal over the next three days, so let's hope you're wrong."

"And you still have to get to Montreal from Toronto."

"That shouldn't be a problem. They run flights almost hourly."

"Spare masks, hand sanitizer, wipes?"

"In a separate Ziploc bag in the outer pocket of my backpack."

"Seriously, I don't know how you fit everything into one backpack carry-on."

"I ditched all that Saxx underwear you bought me in favor of the old fashion reversible kind."

"Ha-ha, very funny. Not."

There was a long pause before she continued, "Mark, you're sure about this?"

This was the big question, wasn't it? On the single sheet of yellow paper was a hypothesis. A hypothesis that postulated a way to cure SARS-CoV-2. Something no one else would think of simply because it was in the realm of the fringe research my dad had been doing for years at the Porton Down Level 4 Containment Labs. A fringe research that remained highly confidential and that ultimately resulted in his retirement when political parties and interests changed. My dad would never discuss it. My only clue had been an article in the paper two decades earlier talking about the protests surrounding Porton Down, where it had been leaked that they were experimenting with weaponized viruses. Apparently, my father had kept his toe in the research pool all these years.

Along with the hypothesis were a number of key references. I had spent all of my free time over the past three days pouring through the literature, nagging our hospital librarian to email me paper after paper. Ultimately, my limited efforts told me that what my dad suggested was possible. Or, at least, not *im*possible. But, really, what did I know? Sure, I had an undergrad degree in microbiology, but that was decades ago. Now, I was an emergency room doctor. The bulk of my practical experience with infectious diseases was prescribing antibiotics for bad pneumonias and pussed-out diabetic toes. Could my dad have stumbled upon a cure for COVID-19? Maybe. But it seemed unlikely.

Still, I had to decide. Not unlike my reckless attempts at "rescuing" Sarah in March, I was forced to weigh options. In this case, I couldn't let even the possibility of a cure for a pandemic that was ravaging the world potentially die with my father. With three million dead and the second wave beginning, there was really no decision to make. I had to try. Even if it meant leaving my pregnant wife to fend for herself.

Sarah convinced me to contact the British authorities, as well as some of my dad's old colleagues at Porton Down.

The British authorities assumed I was a crazed, conspiracy nutjob intent on proving that COVID-19 was a bioweapon designed for the nefarious purposes of: Culling the herd? Establishing a new world order? Other?

At Porton Down, home of the Defence Science and Technology Laboratory, I couldn't get past the secretarial staff. The very mention of my father's name caused an instant hiccup and transfer to "someone in charge," who adamantly insisted that Dr. Spencer no longer worked there and hadn't for many years, and that anything he may have worked on was highly confidential, falling under the Official Secrets Act. Even mentioning that I was his son got me nowhere. I suspect my dad knew that this is exactly what would happen, that his former employment would be unapproachable. He also knew that without the letter he had posted to me, I would never have accepted the ravings of a demented old scientist. He knew that the only way I would brave a transatlantic foray into Britain in this pandemic landscape was if I thought there was a real possibility of a cure. And now, the only way I could know this with any certainty was to go to England.

"Am I sure? Of course not. I'm not sure of anything. But I couldn't live with myself if I didn't try. And, as you've mentioned repeatedly, it's time I reconciled with my father."

If it's not already too late.

Sarah reached over and touched my face. She let out a long sigh as she said, "Sweetheart. I'm just so scared for you."

"I'll be careful. I promise."

"Yes, because you're known as a guy who, in his personal life, is really careful and never takes chances."

"Hey, I only push the limits when love is on the line."

"Hmm. If you say so."

Sarah pulled off Airport Road and onto Dr. Roberta Bondar Parkway. She grinned as she asked, "Did you get a reply from your 'full-time intellect' friend?" Had her hands not been occupied with the wheel, she would most certainly have made air quotes with her fingers.

Understanding the hypothesis and reviewing the references was one thing. Making sense of the various formulae was another matter. I had showed the paper to any colleagues I thought had expertise in this area and had come up empty. No one had any ideas of their validity or how they could possibly relate to a cure for COVID-19. As a last-ditch effort, I sent a scan of the yellow sheet of paper to a new friend. Someone who had proven trustworthy, had a vast knowledge base and was a critical thinker with good pattern making skills. Someone who could get outside the box and put it all together: The Hitchhiker. When we first met, I inquired as to his employment, and he claimed he was a "full-time intellect." He had certainly proven himself to be smart and knowledgeable. I didn't think I had anything to lose by getting his opinion.

"Not yet. He's typically quite erratic in his response time. Could be days or weeks. I'm pretty sure he doesn't have internet and only checks his email when he's near Wi-Fi."

We approached the airport and Sarah slowed down at the exit for departures. She looked at me and then suddenly sped up, passing the exit.

"Sarah, what the hell?"

"I wanted to give you a few more minutes of opportunity to think it over once more. Are you sure you want to do this?"

"You're circling the airport? Like I did for you, right before you jumped on a plane to go to your pharmacy conference in the days before the pandemic was declared?"

"*Quid pro quo*, Doctor."

"Ha. Very funny, Hannibal."

She circled the airport and I fell into deep thought. I reviewed my decision-making process once again. I had approached this decision as I would any medical decision: risk versus benefit. Did the benefits of going to England outweigh the risks? The question was very clear, the answer, however, was still staring at me through a veil of frosted glass. I was getting that weak-kneed feeling again with butterflies bouncing around my insides, like I had when I pushed off from the shores in my kayak in March. I hated being caught in this quicksand of uncertainty.

Sarah pried me out of my thoughts. "What did work say when you told them you were leaving?" She was trying to drive her point home.

"You know what they said. 'We're totally short staffed and, even though we've had only one positive case, the new Covid protocols are killing us. You've been back at work for five days, and you're already leaving again in the middle of your probation period on another crazy adventure? I'm not sure you'll be welcome back this time, Mark.'"

"So, you may not have a job to come home to. Are you ready to give that up?"

Sarah approached the exit, slowed down, looked at me and then sped up again, driving around the airport a second time.

"Another time around?"

"I'll keep going around and around until I know for sure you want this, above all other things."

I had to give her credit. She was making sure that if I stepped onto this path, I would have no regrets. "Sarah, I have to do it. For the sake of my mum, my dad, and God help me, potentially the whole world. What if my doing this allows the discovery of a cure that permits our child to live in a world that has gone back to normal, someday?"

This time around, she pulled onto the departure exit. I had convinced her, and finally, myself. She stopped the truck in front of the departure door, put the vehicle in park and let her shoulders sag. Throughout the drive, she had repeatedly and fleetingly turned her head towards me, looking for all the world like she was never going to see my face again.

"I'm coming back."

Her chin trembled ever so slightly as she whispered, "I know you are. Our baby needs you."

***

The nape of my neck suddenly became damp with perspiration and a knot tightened at the base of my skull. My heartrate accelerated in tandem with the increasing RPMs of the propeller outside my window. I could tell without a mirror that my face had turned pallid white. The flight attendant was making her seatbelt rounds and paused to look at me.

"Dr. Spencer, are you alright?" She had been a patient of mine in the ER during one of her layovers earlier this year, pre Covid. As far as I could recall, she had twisted her ankle on an icy runway walking to the terminal from her plane. She was obviously concerned because her brow was furrowed. Beyond that, her face mask hid most traces of humanity.

"Uhh, I think so. A little nervous, perhaps. The last time I flew things didn't turn out so well." I replied, rubbing the back of my neck.

"Yes, I remember now. The whole Knight in shining armor Covid rescue attempt in Florida. It was in all the papers, even in Toronto."

I bowed my head, not wanting to look her in the eyes. People who knew the story seemed to fall into two camps. Either they thought it was heroic and romantic, or patently stupid and dangerous. I snuck a look. Even through the mask, I could make out the fullness of her cheeks: she was smiling. "Well," she said, "I thought you were very brave. Any woman would be lucky to have a husband so dedicated."

"Thank you. That's very kind."

"You're going to be fine. You've flown many times with us. Try some deep breathing and maybe take a short nap. I'll check on you later. Okay?"

"Sure," I replied, not so sure I was really going to be fine.

The last time I had flown was coming back from Florida with Sarah, after the *ordeal*. Mid-flight, I had developed full-blown fever and chills and later tested positive for COVID-19. In the days that followed, 28 of the 246 souls on that flight also tested positive. I was considered the probable index case for many of them.

Although I never knew the outcome of those 28 individuals, statistically speaking, with a two to three percent mortality rate, one person likely died. That was on me, and it still hurt, *badly*. I was in the business of saving lives, not taking them.

The flight attendant was right, some deep breathing and meditation would be just the thing. I closed my eyes and focused on my breathing just as the captain announced preparations for takeoff. I felt the plane accelerate down the runway and the deep push into my seat. Then, that momentary spike of adrenaline as the wheels left mother earth. The loud hum of the two propeller engines had a comforting, lulling effect, and I felt myself drifting off.

"Can you believe this?" A loud, somewhat nasal voice bellowed in my direction from the seat across the aisle. "Can you?"

Suddenly, I had a pounding headache. I opened my eyes and looked across the aisle taking in the spectacle of a woman that, remarkably, I hadn't noticed when I first sat down. I guestimated she was in her late sixties. She had long silver hair tied into a loose ponytail on the side. Her mask was a flowery scarf drawn across her face – old west, bank robber style. She wore some sort of multi-coloured shawl and, with blue surgical type gloves, was holding an ancient Time Magazine, staring at me, apparently waiting for an answer.

I inhaled deeply and said loudly – because, with the kidney busting propeller engines blazing not twenty feet from my ear separated only by the acrylic plastic of my window, there was no communication onboard without a little yelling, "Can I believe what?"

"All of *this*." She was waving her free hand through the air like a drunk magician, seemingly at a loss for words." And then she stared at me again, waiting for a response. There would be no nap on *this* flight.

"Do you mean all the precautions being taken to prevent the spread of Covid and the unnecessary death of many?" I threw this into the air, a grenade with the pin still in, testing the waters. Nothing that could do real damage but sure to cause some reaction.

"Precautions?" She sat up rigid, straining her seatbelt and placed her Time Magazine into the seat pocket in front of her. "Is that what you call all of this? I call it paranoia. Craziness. I've never …"

I sighed inwardly. *Here we go again.*

"Where are you headed, Ma'am?" I asked, as benign a question as I could think of.

"Back home to Michigan. I've been cooped up at my cottage on a small island near Campement d'Ours since May. It's time to go back to the real world."

"Dual citizenship?" I asked carefully.

"Of course."

Like no one would sneak across the border in times like these. Police boat checks over the summer had been much more common than usual, looking for illegals and smuggling amongst the many islands that lived on Lake Huron in the common waters of the US and Canada where an invisible line in the water separated our two countries. It was interesting that being a dual citizen somehow prevented the coronavirus from spreading across the border. They did have to quarantine for fourteen days after crossing. But did anyone really, completely quarantine for fourteen days?

I said, "I would think the real world would be the last place anyone would want to be right now."

"I don't really have a choice," she replied. "My cottage isn't winterized. It's home to Michigan or freeze to death over the winter."

"Oh. You're on one of the smaller islands with no electricity."

"That's right. It's so beautiful there over the summer. I have a gorgeous garden that I tend and –"

"Wait. You did have internet at your cottage?"

"No, no. Nothing of the sort. That would defeat the purpose of the tranquility of the island, wouldn't it?"

"Cellphone?"

"Yes, of course. For emergencies only, and I never once had to use it." From her purse, she produced an old flip phone.

"And you never left your island, the whole time you were there?"

"Well, with the virus everywhere, I wouldn't dare. After I quarantined for fourteen days it was easy to just stay put. I had a gentleman boat supplies over once a week. I would leave cash in an envelope on the dock. You know, I think he was a little sweet on me. He gave me such looks."

Now it was my turn to sit up in my seat and strain my seatbelt. I leaned closer to her. "So, for the last six months, you've effectively been isolated on a 'deserted island,' by yourself, with no communication to the outside world?"

"Yes. I suppose that's true." She slumped in her seat and looked away to the window.

I shook my head in disbelief. Sarah and I had had this very discussion a few months ago over dinner: *Imagine if you had been marooned on an island since the start of Covid. How different the world would look now. How terrifying it would all feel.*

The airplane levelled off at cruising altitude and the engine RPMs dropped, making speech more reasonable. When the woman turned back to face me, her scarf had dropped down under nose, and I could see that her cheeks were damp. I unbuckled my seatbelt and transferred into the seat next to her. Having been on an isolated island for six months, she was certainly a very low Covid risk. She smiled and said, "It's all so scary."

I nodded my head. "It is. But do you know what the best cure for *scary* is? Knowledge."

She leaned in, tilting her head to one side. "How do you mean?"

"Um," I pointed to her scarf, "Your, um, scarf-mask is slipping."

She immediately pulled it over her nose and then asked, "Seriously? Does it really matter if my nose is sticking out? My mouth is completely covered."

"It does. The Covid virus lives in the back of your nose. If you breathe out through your nose hard enough, you could be exhaling a hailstorm of Covid viruses happy to land on and infect anyone nearby."

The flight attendant appeared at my side. "Dr. Spencer? I see you've found some company. Would you like a beverage?"

"A Ginger Ale would be perfect."

Looking pointedly at my new acquaintance, I asked, "Maybe something for –"

"June. June Fitzpatrick," she said, making eye contact with me and then turning to the flight attendant. "I'm fine. Thank you."

The attendant smiled and then continued down the aisle. I raised my glass slightly in a toasting fashion. "Pleasure to meet you, June."

"And you, Dr. Spencer." There was a short pause before she added, "I guess, as a doctor, you must know a lot about this whole Covid thing?"

"Probably a lot more than I want to. However, as I was saying, the best defense against Covid right now is knowledge, which we get from information."

"Critically appraised and peer reviewed information," I added as an afterthought. "You see, there's a lot of misinformation out there. And there's a lot of information that, while true in the beginning, evolved as new research came to light and is no longer completely true, now."

"How do you mean?"

"Take those gloves you're wearing, as an example." I wiggled my fingers for emphasis.

"These gloves?" she asked. "These are the *very* gloves I wore when I flew to my cottage in May. A nurse friend gave them to me and told me to wear them at all times when I was travelling."

"That was good advice, then. Now, it has been shown that the virus can attach itself to your gloves and from there find its way to your face – your mouth, your nose – and infect you. The current recommendations from the CDC are to *not* use gloves for general outings, including travel. But you must wash your hands repeatedly with soap and water or use an alcohol-based hand wash. Gloves should only be worn when caring for someone who is sick."

June looked first at her gloved hands and then up at me. "You're sure? You're saying I should take these gloves off and just use my hand sanitizer?"

I nodded my head. "That's what the scientific evidence says. And it's what I and all my colleagues do at our hospital. In fact, if you look around at all the other passengers here, very few are wearing gloves. Including the flight attendant."

"Yes. I have to say, I did notice that when I came onboard. And throughout the airport, for that matter." She hesitated for only a second and then removed her gloves, rolling them up and placing them in the airsickness bag. She furled and unfurled her fingers, as if she was seeing them for the first time in a long time. "It feels … dangerous." She then pulled a small bottle of hand sanitizer from her purse and squirted some on each hand, washing them vigorously.

"What kind of doctor are you, Dr. Spencer?"

"I work in the emergency department."

"Then, I guess I can trust that you're up to date on all this Covid stuff. So, tell me, are they working on a vaccine, like for the flu?"

This was the great question on everyone's mind these days as the threat of a second wave and further lockdowns became imminent.

"Yes. There are over a hundred pharmaceutical companies developing vaccines to fight COVID-19. The most promising ones are using completely new technology. Novel technology for a novel virus, I guess you might say."

"How close are we to getting it?"

"Unfortunately, we are still months away. And, when it does come, it will be very complicated to distribute to everyone. You know, who gets it first and all that. Remember, to be effective, since this is a pandemic, the majority of the world has to get the vaccine, and that will take a long time to roll out, no matter how efficient the distribution process. And then, there's the whole matter of how effective it is and whether or not there are any side effects. Only time will reveal those parts of the equation."

"Okay, I guess that's off the table for now." So, what about masks? Do they work against this virus?" As she said this, she sat tall to see over the seats and scan the other passengers. She then slumped confidently back into her chair. "Everyone else seems to be wearing one."

If there was one thing you could count on in times of unknown, it was the comfort of herd conformity – if everyone else is doing what I'm doing then I must be right.

"Masks, masks, masks," I lamented, more to myself than to June. "It's a very controversial topic and one that has created no small amount of division in our society."

"How so?"

"Some believe that masks are not only unnecessary but that they can cause harm to the wearer."

"Can they?" she asked.

"Well, all I can say to that is that surgeons and scrub staff have been wearing masks for generations with no issues."

"The masks are necessary, then, and will protect me?"

"Yes and no."

"How do you mean?"

"The current thinking is that Covid is mostly spread by droplets – that is, if you cough or sneeze, the spittle that's projected into the air will be interlaced with the virus and could land on a surface that someone could touch and become infected or even land on someone's face."

Even through her scarf-mask, I could see that June was making a face. "This is where the six-foot rule came from, I guess?"

"Exactly. The contents of a cough or a sneeze rarely project beyond six feet. So, the rule is: if you are six feet away from people, you don't need a mask. Of course, in some environments, like an airport or a plane, you can't always predict how close people are going to get."

"That's certainly true."

"The virus," I continued, "is also considered an opportunistic airborne. Which means that with certain medical procedures, such as extubating a patient during anesthesia, the virus may be breathed into the air and become airborne, travelling further than six feet and may actually live in the air for unknown periods of time. This is much more dangerous and therefore requires a different kind of mask, a respirator type, like the N95."

"That's the duck-billed one, right?"

"Correct."

"So, as long as I'm not doing medical procedures, which will never happen since I faint at the mere mention of blood, a mask or scarf will protect me."

"Mostly."

"What? You just said –"

June, understandably, sounded frustrated. I was explaining knowledge that had evolved during the last eight months through the publication of over a million scientific papers. This information had then been gradually digested and regurgitated by social media for mass consumption. She was getting it dumped on her in one shot, like a pile of smouldering …

"Hang on, June. Let me explain. It depends what you mean by *protection*. If you mean protection from getting the disease, in the particular case of Covid, standard masks on their own seem to provide limited protection for the wearer. Chances are you'll get infected, but you'll get a lower inoculum."

"You lost me, Doc."

"A lower inoculum means less virus will reach you. Therefore, the disease you get may be less severe, possibly with no symptoms at all. You'll still be contagious in that case – an asymptomatic carrier – able to spread the disease, but you, yourself, won't be sick."

"You're a bit of a techno-talker, aren't you?"

"Sorry. I'm really doing my best to make it understandable for you."

"I think I get it. A regular mask may not prevent me from getting the disease, but if I do get it, it may not be as bad."

"Right. If you think about it, there's lots of room for a virus to get to you around the edges of a standard mask. That's why they have to fit as snugly as possible. In fact, as far as getting infected, it has been shown that masks are more protective for everyone around them than they are for the wearer. The idea is that it keeps any coughs and sneezes contained to the person wearing the mask."

I knew that this concept was something very difficult for a lot of people to grasp. Historically, masks had always been worn to protect the wearer from something in their environment. Although, if anyone gave it some thought, they would realize that, while the mask a surgeon wears is there as physical barrier to prevent the surgeon from getting blood on his or her face, more importantly, it's there to protect the patient's wound from any sneezes or coughs by the surgeon that may contaminate the wound.

"Also, from a filtering perspective, some masks are better than others. Unfortunately, the scarf you're wearing has been proven to be at the bottom of the list relative to the blue surgical types, which have several layers of protection built in and tend to fit more tightly around the face."

"So, I'm not wearing a mask to protect me, so much as I'm wearing it to protect you."

"You got it, Pontiac."

She laughed. "You certainly don't look old enough to remember that commercial."

"A fringe benefit of masks is that they hide some of those nasty aging lines."

"And this scarf I've been wearing isn't all that good for protecting anyone."

"Actually, recent studies have shown that it's not much better than no mask at all."

June shook her head and her shoulders slouched. "You know, I did have a good mask that my nurse friend had given me, but it got ruined in the wash, and I thought the scarf was just as good …"

"Well, it's your lucky day. I happen to have a few spares." I reached across the aisle to my sitting area and dug into my backpack pulling out a Ziploc bag. I retrieved a standard blue mask and gave it to June. She turned her head towards the window, let her scarf fall to her neck and then donned the new mask.

"How do I look?"

"Much safer."

There was a lag in the conversation as June stared out her window once again. She appeared to be thinking hard. After a time, she said, "Everything you've told me, it's a lot to process and a lot to remember."

I paused for a second and then remembered a useful tip I'd been telling my patients. "Well, here's a simple acronym to help. The three 'W's.'"

Her eyes opened wide. She was like a sponge, sucking up everything she could. "Like WWW?"

"Yes. **WWW**:

Wash your hands.

Watch your distance.

Wear your mask."

"I like that: Wash, Watch, and Wear. That's a good one to remember. Thank you."

She turned her face back to the window, obviously deep in thought once again, and then suddenly began shaking her head and pulling on one ear, like she was debating some internal conversation. She faced me once more, this time with a defiant look in her eyes. "Dr. Spencer, I hate to question everything you've told me about wearing a mask, but I have to ask. When I first travelled to my cottage, *He* was saying we didn't need masks, that it was all hogwash."

It took me a moment to zero in on who *"He"* was. She then asked, "I guess *He*'s still in power, isn't he?

It was still hard for me to conceive that she had been so isolated that she had not been exposed to the US political media circus. "Yes, *He*'s very much still in power. And gunning for a second term. *He* has since admitted (well, admitted may not be the right word), or rather, *agreed* that masks are a good thing. *He* wears one himself now, most of the time. He actually tested positive for Covid not long ago and was apparently quite ill. He bounced back with modern medicine."

"Will wonders never cease," was all she could say.

For the remainder of the flight, June enjoyed a crash course on Covid, as well as a little political updating. She proved remarkably perceptive and quick to understand. I wished all my patients could be like her. Nay, I wished all of humanity could be like her. If people were as receptive, as she was, and ready to adopt simple safe practices, as she was, COVID-19 could be defeated.

***

Our plane landed uneventfully in Toronto and rolled to halt on the tarmac adjacent to our gate. Being a smaller plane, there was no passenger boarding bridge. You had to descend a movable set of stairs and then walk outside to the terminal. This could be quite

59

brutal on sub-zero, windy days. As I waited at the front of the cabin to exit the plane, the flight attendant asked, "Feeling better?"

I smiled at her. Even though I knew she couldn't really see it under the mask, I was sure she could sense it. Humans were amazing creatures and capable of decrypting emotions with only the slightest twitch of facial movement, if they wanted to. "Much better. I think I've got that monkey off my back."

"And it looks like you made a new friend." She tilted her head towards June, who needed some extra time and help to disembark.

"Yes, I believe I have." At that moment, I realized that I very much admired June. Six months alone on an island in the middle of all this pandemic, with a bad hip, no less. "She's an extraordinary and courageous woman."

***

June and I had exchanged contact information in the form of email addresses before bidding each other safe travels. I promised to answer any further Covid questions that might come up, if I could. This seemed to give her great comfort, and I felt a little better knowing she was more equipped to deal with the onslaught of the new world that would face her when she arrived in Michigan.

As I entered the terminal, it occurred to me that I had no idea what June looked like. And she had no idea what I looked like. Two complete strangers who had bonded over a one hour flight might pass each other in the street and one might never recognize the other.

That didn't seem right. I stopped in my tracks, much to the consternation of the people around me trying to maintain distance. I checked my watch and noted I was running a little late for the next leg of my journey, but that I should be able to spare a few minutes. When the number of passengers arriving in the terminal tapered off, I turned and ran back outside. This did not sit well with the ground crew.

I yelled, "Forgot something." I spotted June getting off the stairs of the plane with the help of the flight attendant. She was limping badly and was using a cane. I jogged to her and stopped a half dozen feet away.

She looked up, her eyes having been focused on the steps. "Dr. Spencer, did you forget something in the cabin?"

"I believe I did. I forgot to explain one of the crucial rules of etiquette in face mask wearing. It's called *Face Sharing*."

"Face Sharing? Whatever could that be about? It sounds like you made it up."

I dropped my mask below my chin. "It's when two strangers meet for the first time, never having seen each other's face. Six feet apart, they reveal their faces for the other to see in order to bridge the social gap."

June, holding on to her cane with one hand, used her other to lower her mask. She looked much younger than I anticipated. The Great Lakes island life clearly agreed with her. Her skin was clear and bronzed. Her large hazel eyes now made sense in the context of her face, etched with gentle, dynamic laugh lines. We both grinned at each other, like two little kids sitting across from an ice cream Volcano.

"Dr. Spencer, if 'Face Sharing' isn't a real thing, then it should be."

Those were the last words I would ever hear from June Fitzpatrick.

***

The Toronto Pearson Airport was awash with faceless travellers. Masks of every shape and form on display, dancing six feet apart, trying impossibly to obey social distancing as the tide of humanity whirlwinded people to and from their destinations.

How could it be this busy? Where are all these people going? Shouldn't everyone be home, where it's safe?

I stood in front of a men's room fighting the urge. I had just read an article about COVID-19 being spread through the sewage systems of Ottawa. Every time a toilet was flushed, the air was permeated with aerosolized virus. Even if they were cleaning the toilets several times per day, it couldn't protect you from the one person, an asymptomatic carrier, who would do their business and then flush the toilet, sending a potential cloud of COVID-19 into the air of the restroom, air that would be breathed by anyone taking care of their morning routine. There was no safety in social distancing within an aerosolized environment. Was I being paranoid? Of course. But maybe that's how you stayed alive in a pandemic.

I can't hold it forever, or at least, not all the way to England.

Despite the fact that there was no evidence to support the use of a respirator mask in these

62

circumstances, I changed out my regular mask for a duck-billed N-95, designed precisely to protect me against a virus floating through the air, and then entered the men's restroom with trepidation. I was tempted to call out, "Anybody home? Don't flush the toilets. Okay? At least, not until I've gone … and gone."

It was one of the smaller restrooms with maybe a dozen toilets, urinals, and sinks. It looked empty. Still, I crouched down to look under the stall doors, like they do in the movies, looking for the perp. *Who's paranoid?* There was nobody. I bellied up to a urinal and did my business, turning my head from side to side, scanning for intruders. Catching reflections in the various chrome fixtures to see behind me. *There really isn't anybody here.*

I stared at the mirror above the sink into "mine own eyes" as I washed my hands with soap and water. A myriad of emotions radiated from the well of *those* eyes – *my* eyes. There was fear, of course. Fear of travelling and of catching COVID-19 again. Fear of leaving Sarah and our unborn child behind. Fear of losing my job – this time for good. Fear that my father would die, his ideas for a cure – if they even existed – dying with him. Fear that I wouldn't get to him in time to say goodbye and to tell him that, even though he was a jerk most of my life, I still loved him. Fear for a world in trouble, steadily spiralling into the despair of repeated lockdowns, coping with the unbridled emotions of isolation, and teetering on the brink of mental desperation.

But there was also *hope*. Hope that we would all emerge from this pandemic cocoon having discovered something essential about ourselves, as individuals contributing to the web we call humanity. Maybe, this pandemic would somehow make the world a better place?

A bead of perspiration flopped down off my forehead, catching the upper edge of my N95, trying unsuccessfully to work its way in, reminding me that I was fully protected. I took a deep, strained, filtered breath, and then looked at my watch. It was time to catch my next plane. I smiled inwardly as I scanned the empty restroom – there would be no toilet flushing on my watch. I turned and headed for the door, catching a spit of hand sanitizer from a wall unit on my way out, just as all of the toilets and urinals flushed simultaneously, auto timed. I shook my head. Despite every precaution, you just couldn't predict what was going to be around the corner, waiting. You just had to be ready for anything.

***

"How was your flight?" Sarah asked, the phone connection crystal clear for a change.

"No issues," I answered, slaloming around approaching passengers en route to my gate. "A little traumatic flashback from our last flight together, but I met the loveliest elderly woman who kept me completely distracted. Can you believe she isolated on her island near Campement d'Ours for almost six months with no internet or outside contact? She had no idea what was going on in the world."

"Ignorance truly is bliss, I guess."

"Don't worry," I said. "Her bliss was soundly trampled by my pack of information hounds."

"Couldn't help yourself, eh?"

"Information is protection, right?" I dodged an oncoming golf cart filled with older passengers wearing summer gear apparently heading to sunny, southerly, non-US destinations. Costa Rica, maybe? Their borders were still open to travellers. A pang of jealously ricocheted through my chest. Wouldn't it be nice to go lie on a beach somewhere with Sarah for a week? It had been more than a year since we travelled anywhere fun. Florida this past March definitely didn't qualify as fun.

"Hmm, I suppose," Sarah said. "There is such a thing as information overload, though."

"Maybe." I responded, thinking one person's overload might be another's happy place, and too much was better than too little.

Sarah continued, "That was a fairly terrible metaphor, by the way – information hounds."

"They can't all be gems, my love. Speaking of hounds, how's –"

"– Bugger!" I had just jumped onto a high speed moving walkway and was doing a slow trot when a business type ran through on my left. In that instant of reflexively trying to avoid contact, I nearly went over the side. *That was way too close, arsehole.*

"How's … *bugger*?" Sarah asked.

"Sorry. Some business lady in a hurry severely infringed upon my personal, Covid-free space. Didn't even get a sorry from her."

"Sounds like a battle zone at Pearson Airport."

I was straightening out my backpack which had gone awry. "Yeah, a little bit. Anyway, I was asking how Archie was."

"Well, since you've only been gone for a few hours, I'm pretty sure he hasn't noticed your absence, yet."

"Hey, dogs can sense those kinds of things."

"Hmm, I suppose."

I was making good time getting to my next gate, alternating from one moving walkway to the next. As I rounded a corner, holding the shoulder strap of my backpack with one hand and my phone with the other, I came across a most unexpected site.

"Whoa," I said to Sarah as I came to a full stop. "You won't believe what I'm looking at."

"Tell me."

"Well, speaking of dogs that can sense, I'm looking at a roadblock of three dogs and their handlers set up at three stations. They're each standing in front of a sign that says 'COVID-19 testing' with a dog sporting a blue vest with a white cross on it underneath. Hang on, I'll message you a pic ..."

There was a short pause before Sarah squealed, "Ooh, they're so cute. They look like the drug dogs at customs, but without the attitude. One of them looks just like Archie. Are you going to do it?"

I was about to say "yes," but then, my scientific mind took over. I quickly googled "Covid sniffing dogs" and came up with a slew of hits. I read some highlights: the program had just started in Helsinki and was quickly spreading across the world. Currently in the testing phase, it still wasn't mandatory for passengers. I assumed it was on trial at Pearson Airport. One article described how the dogs would sniff a special cloth that had been wiped across the test subjects' neck or back of hand. Although the dogs had been 100% accurate in their results so far, one article did mention that the dogs could become fatigued by the constant overload of complex human smells. What if I was tested by a tired dog who had been sniffing all day and produced a rare false positive? It would turn into a circus. At the very least, I would be put in isolation pending an official test and who knows how long it would take to get the result. I would certainly miss my flight and I couldn't take the chance.

"I'm going to have to pass. Running to catch my flight."

"Ahh, too bad," Sarah said. "Would've made a good story. Maybe I'll train Archie to sniff out Covid while you're away. That way I'll know you're 'clean' when you come home."

"Ha. Funny girl. Good luck with that. I was barely able to train Archie to sit."

"That's because Archie's smarter than you." The conversation suddenly hit a wall. While Sarah was partly joking, the tone of her voice suggested that she was also partly serious. She was taking a subtle, deep dig.

"Thanks. Despite all your reassuring words, you're still pissed at me for leaving, aren't you?"

"What? That the husband of my unborn child has gone traipsing across the globe in the middle of a pandemic second wave?"

"It's not a real second wave … yet, and you forgot the part about my dying father and possibly a clue to the cure for the pandemic."

Sarah let out a lengthy sigh. "Mark. Allow a pregnant woman to feel a little narcissistic for a moment, would you? Now that you're gone, the house feels … empty."

"You know I feel terrible leaving you."

There was a short pause as she, hopefully, absorbed my sincerity. She then switched gears and asked, "Do you think you'll hear anything more from your mother?"

"She said, 'no news is good news.' I'll hold her to that statement. If everything goes as planned, I should be there late tomorrow morning …"

Famous last words.

***

The floor surrounding the gate entrance for my connecting flight to Montreal looked like the chalk filled playground of a grade school. There were multicolored lines directing passengers where to stand and where to walk. Unlike the chaotic frenzy in the rest of the airport, there seemed to be fewer travellers here. Likely the recent surge in Québec's Covid numbers had something to do with it. Travel these days was influenced as much by risk as by necessity. The overhead speaker emanated a continuous stream of instructions voiced by a woman with a calming French accent. I joined the queue, hopping ever so slowly six feet from one designated "X" on the floor to the next in a ratchety, unpredictable way that reminded me of being online for a Disney ride.

During one of the more prolonged moments of stasis, I reflexively pulled my phone from the breast pocket of my jacket and glanced at a blank screen. *Fuck.* I had chatted with Sarah for another ten minutes as I walked towards my departure gate and then my phone had died in the middle of our conversation. Somehow, the battery power had gone from 90% to zero in the space of an uttered word. *Fixed my ass. Bloody technology, it works just long enough to create expectations and then – poof! – disappointment.*

When it was finally my turn at the ticket counter, a masked and shielded airline employee asked me the usual barrage of screening questions, much like I'd been asked on two occasions when I boarded my first flight. After I stepped forward to the next "X," another employee checked my temperature with a temple scan. She nodded and then indicated I could show my boarding ticket to the next agent. I sanitized my hands and, of course, this is when I produced my dead phone and realized I didn't have a printout, wanting to save a few trees and decrease the exchange of potentially contaminated paper.

Damn. I'm screwed.

I explained the situation to the agent, who may have frowned at me – difficult to say for sure with the full facial coverage – and then pointed to a seat next to the counter with a plug nearby. I pulled my charger from my pack and immediately plugged in … and waited.

The line quickly trickled down to one person. My phone remained blank. Evidently, my phone had a new problem, a defective battery that was on its last legs. There wasn't time to run to the Air Canada ticket outlet, which was a solid half kilometer from my current position. Praying was perhaps too strong a word, but I definitely reached out to some higher technological power. My phone answered with a burst of red battery emblem on the screen. A good sign but still not the access I needed to my digital wallet, where my ticket was hiding.

The last passenger made her way down the gangway and all three agents – the ticket-agent, the screening-agent and the "thermo?"-agent – turned their heads to look at my embarrassed, ticketless self.

"Sir? You have five minutes."

I looked at my phone and willed it to come alive. And it did. I suppressed a victory cry and quickly found my electronic ticket. It was hard not to do an NFL type, touchdown-scoring dance, wiggling my ass for the cameras with a "Yeah, I just did that" kind of attitude. Instead, with great determination and focus, I sucked in a deep breath and calmly showed the ticket agent my barcode displaying phone. I then walked down the gangway with my backpack slung over my shoulder and forced myself not to look back.

***

Apparently, the social distancing rule is completely nullified when you board a plane. My sense of urgency was completely discarded when I saw the crushing line of people squirming to find an overhead compartment to stow their carry-on bags and then locate their seats. I had researched this extensively – *Where was the safest place to sit on a plane?* Not from the perspective of a crash (the tail) but from the perspective of not catching a disease (the newer, much more real threat).

Research has determined that an airplane, with its HEPA filters and ventilation system working to completely exchange the air up to 12 times per hour in the cabin, is one of the safest places to breathe, much safer than an average building. By the same token, the ventilation system only fires up once the doors are closed, and pressurization begins. The corollary to this was that the most dangerous part of flying – from an infection perspective – was in the moments passengers were boarding. The safest thing you could do was make a beeline to your seat with your mask on and stay there. At that point, once the ventilation fired up, you were exposed only to the people next to you or in seats in front or behind. The HEPA filter would take care of everyone else's infectious expectorate onboard.

I found my window seat and removed a couple of Virox wipes from my backpack before shoving it under the seat in front of me. I wiped down everything within reach. Once I was satisfied that I'd created a veritable aseptic sanctuary, I felt all of my achy travel muscles loosen and knots that had been welded into my traps suddenly melt. I plugged my miserable phone into an outlet, hoping the one-hour flight would give it enough juice to be functional in Montreal. I then looked around and noticed that, as per CDC recommendations, every second seat on the plane was purposefully left empty. All was safe in my bubble, until the man with the black, one-way valve mask sat down in the seat next to me.

***

Had it not been covered, I'm sure the surprise on my face would've made him think twice. As it was, he settled in comfortably with pre-Covid behavior, oblivious to my presence. There was no attempt to sanitize anything; it was business as usual. And he did, indeed, look like a high-powered businessman, wearing a very expensive suit and tie with highly polished shoes that glared like his completely hairless cranium. His black mask was unusual in that it also had a visor extending from it as well as neck coverage. I was annoyed and intrigued.

"Umm, Sir?" I pointed my index at his seat and then at the aisle seat next to him, as if swiping on a phone repeatedly, magically trying to push him away from me. He turned to me, and, through the visor, I could see his eyebrows rise like two little mountain peaks.

"Sorry?" he asked.

"I'm pretty sure this airline has an open middle seat policy," I stated bluntly.

"Does it? He looked around the cabin and obviously realized that all of the middle seats were empty. "Oh. I had no idea. The last flight I was on, connecting to this one, didn't have that policy."

"Would you mind if I stayed in this middle seat?" he continued. "I have a tendency to tilt to the right, a bit of scoliosis, you know. I hate getting jostled by everyone going back and forth. Not to mention the beverage cart."

"Uhh," was all that came out of my mouth before an overhead announcement saved me.

"Ladies and gentlemen, please note that we are travelling with an empty middle seat policy on this flight. No passengers are permitted in the middle seats."

I looked at him, shrugged my shoulders, pointed to the speaker above our seats and said, "Sorry."

He sighed and then slowly changed seats. Under his breath, he muttered, "Damn Covid BS."

Once he was settled, he dropped his tray and placed his laptop on it. He was about to remove his mask when another announcement was made, "Ladies and gentlemen, please note that this is only a one-hour flight, and it is required that you keep your masks on at all times unless you need to eat or drink. Please note that no food or beverage will be served on this short flight."

"Aww, geez," he said, loud enough for several passengers to hear as he repositioned his mask.

In an effort to break the tension, I commented, "I'm curious about your mask. It seems awfully … decked out."

"This mask is top shelf. Considered 99% effective in protecting from Covid." He suddenly became very engaged, and his chest expanded just a little. He leaned in and pointed to his face as he said, "In fact, this is one of my masks. It's my business."

"You're a …," I wasn't quite sure what to say. "You're a mask engineer?"

"Salesman," he corrected. "I have a friend who designs them. I sell them."

"And … sales are good?" I asked.

"Very. At this rate, I'll be able to retire next year."

I was in my forties with retirement still decades away. He looked to be early thirties at most. Business was clearly *very good.*

"Umm, what about that exhalation filter on the mask? You know, it's a one-way valve." I could tell from the construct that it really was nothing more than a plastic one-way valve with no filters. "Everything you're breathing out is going into the air. That mask is only protecting *you*."

"That's the idea, isn't it? To protect yourself."

"Well, not really. The reason it's mandated is to protect everyone around you from possible contaminants in your exhalation. Particularly, if you're an asymptomatic carrier."

"Whatever," he said, sitting back heavily in his seat. "I'm making a fortune with this mask. It has this wicked neck protection as well as the visor." He waved his hands over the different parts of his mask as he described them in a Vanna White type manner.

"Yes. I see that, but –"

"Look, we both know that a lot of this Covid stuff is bullshit, right? Might as well make some money off it while we can?"

Covid bullshit? Flashbacks from my first meeting with The Hitchhiker eight months earlier popped into my head. *Another non-believer? Or was he?* I would try a different approach.

"You're not afraid of getting Covid? A disease that has killed over a million people worldwide?"

"Hey, if I get it again, I get it again. It wasn't pleasant the first time around, but I got through it, just like most others. Can't live with my head in the sand forever."

"You've already had it?"

"Seven months ago, in early April. I was coming back from a sales pitch overseas. It wasn't so bad. And they say the second time around is easier. I'd just as soon get the second wave now and get it over with."

He wanted to get the virus?

"It's not really a second wave, more like a second peak," I corrected him.

"Whatever, that's not what the newsfeeds are saying."

"A second wave implies that the first wave has petered out and a new mutated version of the virus is on the loose. Since most people have still not gotten the virus, this is just a second peak."

"Again, whatever. To-may-to, to-mah-to. If they say it's a second wave, then that's good enough for me and good for business."

"You don't really care, then, if it's really a second wave?"

"Hey, as long as the virus is making the news – giving me free publicity – and demand for my product continues to skyrocket, they can call it whatever the hell they want. Don't get me wrong, I care about people, but business is business."

And then it hit me, *the man with the black mask was a modern-day profiteer.*

Still, I couldn't believe he didn't care about getting the virus again. I had been through it, and it was the most miserable experience I'd ever had in my life.

"You know," I said, "there's evidence that, for some people, once they've had this virus, it causes chronic changes in their lungs and vascular system. A second hit could be worse than the first, maybe even kill them."

"What are you? A doctor or something?"

"Emergency doctor in a small town in Northern Ontario."

"That explains it. You see the sickest people all the time, so you think the worst of everything and act like everyone has it. It's all you think about."

He wasn't wrong on this point. Even though only one true case had been identified in our hospital, the operations of hospital life were affected every second of every day: front line workers being forced off work with the sniffles or, really, any symptom of a common cold; primary care givers required to wear costly and cumbersome personal protective equipment for patient contacts; housecleaners required to do lengthy cleaning procedures for rooms or places where patients had been; waiting rooms modified to accommodate social distancing and flow. The list of changes at the hospital level was innumerable and we received regular updates on everything Covid all the time. It really *was* mostly all we thought about.

"That's true," I admitted. "It doesn't change the facts, though. It could be lethal."

"Sure, Doc. Don't me wrong, I'm as scared of dying as the next guy, but I'm probably more likely to die in a plane crash than from Covid, especially since I have some immunity now."

"Not sure that's accurate. The death rate worldwide is sitting at 4% at the moment."

"That's mostly for older people and, between you and I," he winked at me, "it's the number I tell my potential clients to get them to buy. The reality is that, at my age, with no risk factors, I have a better chance of getting hit by lightning than dying from Covid."

His points were all valid.

"Okay, even if you only get a mild version, maybe even no symptoms, aren't you worried about giving it to your loved ones. Maybe they have risk factors that you don't. Maybe they're more vulnerable."

"To be honest, I don't really have any loved ones I'm in contact with regularly. I'm single with no kids. My grandparents have all passed away. My parents are divorced and live in other parts of the world. Don't get me wrong, I care about transmitting the virus to others, but, as long as I don't have the virus, I can't pass it on, right?"

"Of course, but how do you know you don't have it? Even right now?"

"First of all, I get tested weekly because of all the travel I'm doing. Secondly, I follow all of the precautions: sanitizing my hands, wearing this outstanding mask, limiting by bubble. Thirdly, I know what it feels like since I've had it before. And, I don't have it."

"Did you lose your smell and taste?" I licked my lips as I said this, thinking back to my experience.

"Yeah, it took a month to get it back." He paused as he looked me over. "The way you said that, it sounded like you were speaking from experience."

"Last March, down in Florida. It was 37 days before I could enjoy a glass of wine again."

"Ha. Looks like we're kindred spirits."

Not quite.

"You have no qualms about making money off of other people's misery."

"No offense, Doc, but you make a living out of other people's misery. If there was no disease, you'd have no job."

"Yes, but … but it's not the same. You said it yourself. You're capitalizing on other people's fear of Covid to sell them masks."

"Sure, but they need masks, don't they? It's practically a law. I'm just providing them with options to upscale to a better product. They don't have to buy *this* mask."

"You can't prove your mask is better. There's no scientific evidence to back up your claims."

"I never said my mask was better. Just cooler. More dope, as youngsters would say. In fact, three quarters of my sales are in the 16 to 25 age-group."

"And the other quarter?"

"Mostly elderly."

"They're just looking for what they think is the best possible protection since, for them, the disease could be lethal," I pointed out.

"No doubt. And you have to admit, with the visor and the neck guard, it's pretty good protection."

"I guess. But there's still the matter of the one-way valve."

"Tell you what. Maybe I can talk to my designer about putting a HEPA filter in. Next level stuff. More expensive version."

This man had an answer for everything. I was frustrated because a lot of what he was saying was true, and yet, it didn't ring right. It didn't feel right. It felt dirty. Had Covid really become just another commodity to be taken advantage of? Another business opportunity? That didn't seem right. Once again, I felt all of *my* convictions being watered down by someone who was just going about their life and living it according to *their* convictions and circumstances. *Live and let live, I guess.*

***

We both settled in for an uneventful flight. I snoozed intermittently, my thoughts in turmoil as I hashed through my conversation with the man in the black, one-way valve mask, looking for loopholes in his arguments. It turned my stomach to meet someone who really didn't care about the greatest pandemic of the last hundred years. Correction, he did care about the business opportunity it presented, but not about the devastation to humanity that would result. On the one hand, he was like an arms dealer profiteering from a war in another country. On the other, he really *wasn't,* since he was providing much needed protection, although at a price. I really didn't know what to make of him. I supposed he was just a human making his way through this new world as best he knew how. Who could blame him for that?

The plane jarred as the wheels hit the runway, shaking me back to reality. I looked over at my "antagonist" and he simply said, "Good flight? You were passed out pretty hard there. Mustn't have slept much last night. Hey, I never asked why you were flying? I spend a lot of time in the air and haven't met many medical people. With all the quarantine rules, they usually keep pretty close to home."

And just like that, with a few simple, empathetic questions, the enemy of my dreams transmorphed into a regular guy. It took me a few seconds to bring him into focus. It didn't feel like it, but perhaps I *was* out for the duration. He had hit the nail on the head. Sleep had been difficult to come by these past few days with my brain all tied up in decision-making knots.

I rubbed my eyes, sat up straighter in my seat and considered my response for a second before saying, "My dad's dying from Covid. I'm travelling to England to be with him and my mum."

"Ouch. That's terrible. I'm really sorry to hear that. I figured your travels were family related. Most peoples are these days. Montreal to England is a long flight, and it's probably the red eye, so you're going to have to kill quite few hours since it's only," he looked at his watch, "noon now."

He shuffled through his briefcase and pulled a sheet of paper. "Listen, I've accumulated a zillion points from spending so much time in the air. That comes with a few perks. Take this," he passed the sheet of paper to me, "it will get you into the Gold Lounge. Sleeping pods, free food and, best of all," he raised his eyebrows, "free cocktails."

"That's, umm, incredibly generous of you."
Damn him and his kindness.
"It's my pleasure. You guys on the front lines deserve any perks you can get. Plus, you gave me that idea for the HEPA filter upgrade. I'll make a ton on that."

We pulled into the gate to the sound of unclicking seatbelts and the buzzing of phones coming alive. I realized we hadn't formally introduced ourselves. The man in the black mask was standing in the aisle already, his carry-on at his side.

I made eye contact and extended my knuckles to him. "Apologies. I never introduced myself. Mark Spencer."

He extended his knuckles and bumped mine. "Pleased to meet you, Dr. Spencer. I'm Charlie Treemont. My friends call me Chuck."

"Pleasure to meet you, Chuck. Have you ever heard of Face Sharing?"

"Can't say as I have. Something like FaceTime or Facebook?"

"A little. It's when two appropriately distanced strangers drop their masks for a moment in order to see each other's faces."

I lowered my mask and then he did the same, revealing a broad smile with shiny white teeth surrounded by a goatee. He reminded me of a skinnier version of the animated Burl Ives in the Christmas classic, Rudolf the Red Nosed-Reindeer, and he instantly emanated this incredibly infectious *joie de vivre*. I could see why he would be such a good salesman. With that face, I would practically buy anything from him.

"Face Sharing," he said, scratching his head. "That's brilliant, Doc. You've just given me another million-dollar idea. See-through masks. Brilliant. Here, take my card. You have to contact me if you have any other great ideas."

I smiled and tucked his card into my wallet. Apparently, I'd somehow become complicit in his profiteering. The world worked in mysterious ways.

***

I checked my phone as I entered the airport and noticed a message from Sarah that said, "CALL ME. Urgent. 2 things."

Capital letters, "call me"? That's never good.

I had eight hours and change to kill before boarding my flight to London. I immediately sat down in a nearby seat with no one around and tapped her name. My phone was registering a one hundred percent charge, for now. She answered almost before I could get my phone to my ear.

"Mark?"

I've always found it fascinating that, even though I know my name just popped up on Sarah's screen, and she absolutely knows it's me, she still has to ask. Old habits.

"Yes, it's me, Sarah, I just landed in Montreal. What's so 'capital letters' urgent?"

"Your mother's been trying to reach you. I was walking Archie, and there was a message on the answering machine when I got back."

"Why didn't she call my cell?"

"Maybe she did. Have you checked your voicemail?"

I swiped here and there, looked at my screen and, sure enough, a red dot was glowing next to the voicemail icon, two reels of an antiquated tape deck with a thin spool of tape between them.

"Damn, you're right. She left a message. She never leaves a message. You called her back? What did she say?"

"Just contact her right away, Mark. It sounds like your dad has taken a turn for the worse."

"Okay. Before I do that, what's the second thing?"

She sighed heavily before she replied, like wind blowing through an overpass, "I know you haven't had a chance to check the news. It sounds like the second wave has hit the UK hard. There are talks about shutting down their borders again. Are you sure your flight is still on?"

I stood from my seat and locked on to the closest departure screen. I shouldered my backpack and marched towards it, my mind already looking for a contingency plan and coming up empty. I scanned through the flights until I found the Montreal – London. I smiled and pressed my phone to my ear. "It says it's on time, departing at 9 PM."

"That's good, Mark." Her voice wavered. She didn't sound convinced, either that the flight would go as planned, or that it was in any way *good*. "Keep a close eye on it, though. Things could change at any moment."

"Will do, Sarah. I promise." My stomach gurgled and I realized it was lunchtime. "Hey, long story, but the guy next to me on this last flight gave me a voucher for the Gold Lounge. I'm going to head over there to grab a bite and kill some time."

"You're just meeting all sorts of fun people, aren't you?"

"I suppose I am. I'll probably get stuck next to a morbidly obese snoring machine on the next flight."

Sarah laughed and then said, "Call your mother, now."

"I hear you, Cap'n. Love you."

"Love you, too, sailor boy."

***

I was about to call when I realized the news could be bad, really bad. I needed some privacy. I decided that a pod in the Gold Lounge would the perfect place and headed straight there. I hunched forward, eyes to the floor, with that juggernaut stance that radiated to everyone around me, "coming through and you'd best step aside if you don't want to get stampeded."

In short order, I stood in front of the Gold Lounge reception where an attendant with a smiley face motif mask looked over my voucher and ushered me through. I had never been in the Gold Lounge before, but it only took seconds to locate the infamous pods that I'd heard so much about from my more worldly and wealthy friends. They were very much like the pods found on first class international flights. Completely self-contained and enclosed recliner chairs equipped with full AV and some kind of noise reduction system. I settled in, noting the fresh scent of disinfectant and feeling a damp spot where the plush leather had recently been wiped, and then immediately dialed my mother's land line. If hospitals in London were anything like home with current Covid protocols, there would be no visitors allowed, and, as such, there was really no other place my mother could be. After three rings, she picked up.

"Hello?"

"Mum, it's Mark. What's happening?"

There was an unusually long pause before my mother spoke which immediately turned my guts to stone. My mother was typically sharp as a tack and quick as a rattler on the phone. There was never any wasted time. "Your father has taken a turn for the worse. They had to put him on a ventilator this morning."

I did the calculations in my head. It was approaching 1 PM in Montreal, now. So, 8 PM in England. This happened maybe ten hours, or so, ago. "I thought he was better. I thought you said he was more lucid and talking?"

"He was, Mark. In fact, they allowed me a phone call with him this morning. He went on and on and wouldn't stop talking, like he knew he had only this one opportunity to get it all out."

"What did he say?" My dad knew everything about infections, clinical courses, recovery, and relapses. *What do you say if you think it's the last time you'll ever say anything?*

"He said he had spent his life's work trying to kill the little buggers and this was their revenge. He really opened up, like I'd never heard him. He talked about our life together. He said he didn't regret all the hours he'd put in at work but if, somehow, there were more hours in the day, he would have spent every one of them with me …" There was a muffled silence, as if she'd put her palm over the phone receiver. When she began speaking again the words were interrupted by gentle sobs. For the first time that I could remember, she sounded like a frail old woman who was about to lose her soulmate.

"As you know, your father is not normally one to openly express his emotions. He told me repeatedly that he loved me."

That sure doesn't sound like the father I know.

She continued, "He was talking about you. How proud he was. How much he wished he had grandchildren –"

"Did you tell him Sarah is pregnant?"

"I was about to when he started coughing and became short of breath. I could hear the nurse trying to pull the phone from him, and he was fighting her. Then it was like he suddenly became a scientist again. A mad, delirious scientist, laughing between coughing fits. He kept saying the little buggers may get him, but he would have the last laugh. He said to tell you not to disappoint him. At all cost, you must come to England. It was all in his lab. Everything you needed to change the course of this pandemic. To save millions of lives …"

That sounds more like my father.

"He kept saying 'do not disappoint, do not disappoint,' over and over again until the nurse finally wrestled the phone away from him. I could hear him struggling to catch his breath. The line went dead, but later a doctor called me back. She told me they had to sedate him and place him on a ventilator. They repeated a CT scan and said his lungs were full of something that sounded like glass, I couldn't really understand what they meant."

They meant GGO or Ground Glass Opacifications. These were descriptive findings on CT scan often associated with Covid. Hazy white flecked markings seen in the lobes of the lungs. Not necessarily a bad sign on its own unless it was combined with other findings like blood tests, age, other imaging findings and comorbidities. Then it could indicate a poor prognosis for recovery.

"Mum, it means his lungs are full of the Covid virus." My mother wasn't a medical person but, between my dad and I, she had picked up some of the lingo over the years. She also wasn't someone to beat around the bush. She didn't need kid gloves. "It means his prognosis is not very good."

"I know, Mark. I understand that much." There was a pause and it sounded like she was drinking something – likely a cup of Twining's English Breakfast Tea, her favorite.

She continued, "Sarah said you would be here tomorrow morning."

"That's right, Mum. I expect I'll be home just before lunch." Home was a large Victorian style house in Southampton that my parents had purchased over sixty years ago. My bedroom was still as I left it when I moved to Canada to study medicine at McGill. They had changed nothing.

"That's good, Mark. I'm anxious to see you and put this envelope matter to rest, one way or another. Your father said you would know what to do."

My days in the lab were eons ago, during my undergrad degree at Oxford. I wasn't so confident I would know what to do with whatever I found. If I found anything.

"Would it not make more sense to get some of dad's old colleagues involved. People who really knows what they're doing?" I asked.

"I called two of his old workmates from Porton Down that I hadn't seen in many years. They laughed at the notion that your dad could have discovered a cure. They laughed and called him a crazy old fool still living in his glory years. Your dad was very specific before he went to the hospital and, now more than ever, I'd like to respect his wishes. No one but you is to be allowed in his lab. Only you can access his safe, and only you can understand his work."

I remained perplexed. I couldn't imagine what current knowledge I possibly had that qualified me to interpret my dad's scientific discoveries.

There was suddenly a buzzing noise in the pod with a blinking red light that apparently meant there was an important overhead announcement.

"I have to go, Mum. Listen, Dad's as stubborn as they come. He won't let the little buggers get him. I'll see you tomorrow morning, okay?"

I would definitely not see my mother the following morning.

***

I remember ...

My butt was aching after sitting on the wooden chair outside the principal's office for what seemed like eternity. Finally, my mother arrived, and we were escorted in.

"Mum," I whispered, "where's dad? He's supposed to be here."

She shook her head.

I was placed on a hard stool in the corner, while my mother was seated in a leather upholstered chair directly across from Mrs. Fisher's desk. She was looking down at a dossier and grimacing. Her face was pointy, exactly like a fish, and her grey streaked hair was pulled back as tight as a fishing line holding a hundred-pound Marlin. I wasn't particularly fond of her before this disciplinary meeting, and I would downright hate her afterwards. She had a framed picture of her family resting in an angled way on her desk. From where I was sitting, I could just make out her husband and two kids. They all looked like fish.

"Mrs. Spencer, Mark's behavior was highly irregular. For a ten-year-old-boy to go traipsing across town on his own in the middle of a school day for no other reason than to buy a – she looked at her dossier again – to buy a Mars chocolate bar is unacceptable. He apparently left the school at recess, walked through the field, then along a motorway and, finally, hitchhiked a ride to Frederick's Chocolates. A grand adventure that was very dangerous … and highly irregular."

She turned her head and looked at me with those big fishy eyes. "What do you have to say for yourself, young man?" My mother turned to look at me as well.

I stood up and stepped forward to the desk, my arms were tightly crossed over my chest, which was thumping along like I'd run the mile. "Isn't my father supposed to be here, also?"

Mrs. Fishface turned to my mother. "Where is Dr. Spencer?"

"I'm afraid he was detained at Porton Down. Some sort of breakthrough." Everyone in Southampton knew about Porton Down. It carried an aura of prestige and mystique that sparked rumors and controversy daily, particularly in regard to national security.

"I certainly understand, Mrs. Spencer."

I stiffened noticeably and opened my mouth, but nothing came out. Until it did. "But he's supposed to be here. The school rules say that both parents have to be here for a discip … disciplin … disciplinarian meeting. I read them. On the sheet *you* circulated at the beginning of the school year. I read them. He has to be here."

"Now, Mark," my mother said calmly, "sometimes we have to make exceptions. Your father is doing important work. It's the middle of the day. He can't be expected to come –"

I yelled, "He's never expected to be anywhere …"

It wasn't intentional, or maybe it was. I'm not sure. In trying to express myself, and get my point across, like lawyers in a courtroom on the telly, my arms flew open and one hand smacked Mrs. Fishface's family photo. It soared across the room and smashed against the wall, the glass and frame clattering to the floor in pieces.

At first, I stood rock still. Not understanding what I'd just done. And then my legs turned to jelly, and I fell onto my mother's lap and started sobbing uncontrollably.

I was given 64 days of detention at school and grounded for the same amount of time at home. I saw my dad only once during that time. I was nodding off to sleep a few days after the "event," when my dad poked his head in through my bedroom door.

"Mark, you're quite a spirited young lad, aren't you?" he whispered. "Don't do it again."

It was dark, but I think he was smiling. It was worth all 64 days.

***

A Covid Odyssey Second Wave

I exited the pod, holding my backpack in one hand and my phone in the other, and joined a gathering of people in front of two large LCD screens: one for departures and the other for arrivals. It occurred to me that a number of people here weren't just waiting for flights to leave, they were waiting for loved ones, business partners, and friends to arrive. Another perk of wealth or good fortune was waiting in a very comfortable environment.

Through the murmur of masked voices, slow and steady like the tide, I could feel the rising anxiety and the collective holding of breaths. While a number of people were staring at the airport LCD screens, others were standing in front of TV news screens, or leaning against a wall simply scrolling their phones. Although everyone was digging for information in their own particular, individual ways, one thing we all had in common was that we were standing.

My eyes were fixed on the airport departure screen, waiting for the international flights. At first, all the UK flights were noted to be on time. And then, the dreaded "cancelled" appeared progressively from top to bottom, as if someone had just thrown a switch to purposefully derail everyone's plans. A number of whispered swear words escaped with the release of held breaths as rigid bodies turned away from the screens. Earbuds were pushed deeper into eardrums, or phones were pushed harder into the sides of faces, as cell towers became overloaded with a waterfall of desperate calls. We'd all been *covided*!

I scrolled through my phone and confirmed what Sarah had said: the UK and several European countries had closed their borders to international flights. It was now official. As with the first wave, while there might be intermittent flights allowing UK citizens to return home, citizens without UK passports would not be allowed entry. At that very moment, I cursed my idiocy for not having a dual citizenship passport. Although I had spent my childhood raised in Southampton, I was born in Montreal when my father was on sabbatical teaching at McGill for three years. Although my parents had obtained a dual passport for me when we returned home, I purposefully let it lapse after I moved to Canada and married Sarah. I wanted all connections to my father severed.

I called Sarah immediately.

"So, you're coming home?" Restrained happiness leaked around the edges of her voice.

"I don't see any alternative. Do you?"

"Maybe wait and see if they lift the border restrictions?"

After the first wave, it was months before flying restrictions were eased, and Sarah knew that. She was trying to be supportive, but there was no reason to think it wouldn't be as long or longer this time. "We will likely have a newborn baby by the time that happens."

Simmering beneath our conversation, I was being riddled by the arrows of a dozen conflicting emotions. Anger at having my mission derailed – *covided.* Grief for my mother and father. Disappointment at not being able to verify my dad's hypothesis. Guilt for not having put things right with my father. And even greater guilt for the millions of deaths that might have been avoidable had I been able to bring my father's cure into the light – if it proved to be real.

But I also had gratitude that I could return home to Sarah and back to the job I loved. Ultimately, an overwhelming sense of relief flooded my mind and heart. I had nothing to be guilty about; I had given it my best shot.

Or had I?

"My mother sounded so desperate. She'll be crushed to hear that I'm not coming. And it's possible I'll never see my father alive again." As I continued talking to Sarah, I wandered over to a table in the bar area, threw my backpack on it and slouched into a comfortable lounge chair. It was like I'd lost a race I never had the chance to run.

"There's nothing you can do, Mark. It's not like you can swim there."

Little did Sarah suspect the foretelling ring of truth that her words would hold.

***

In the end, I told Sarah that I would catch the next available flight home, but first, I would call a few travel agents to see if there were any other options.

There were none.

All international travel off the continent was on hold. And as far as returning home, I quickly discovered that I wasn't the only traveller in this predicament. The earliest top dollar flight I could find wouldn't leave until the following evening. I had to spend the night in Montreal. Not such a bad thing under the circumstances. It would, perhaps, give me a chance to come to grips with everything as well as allow some time to think about how I was going to break it to my mother. Maybe I could call another of my dad's old Porton Down scientist colleagues and see if a master key to the safe still existed, although, thirty or more years later, that seemed unlikely. And, even if it did exist, it would probably be buried so deep in bureaucracy that it may as well not exist at all.

A waitress approached and asked if I wanted anything off the menu. Although initially I refused, stubbornly thinking that I should be busy trying to find a way to England or home instead of sitting back and enjoying myself like I was on holidays, ultimately, I put the guilt aside and gave in. What else did I have to do at the moment? I ordered a locally made craft beer and a classic Montreal smoked meat sandwich – both favorites since med school.

As I pulled my eyes from my phone, already at 30% charge and dropping rapidly – *bloody smartphone* – I inhaled deeply and, for the first time, took a good look around the Gold Lounge. An air of tension was palpable as travellers attempted to change their plans. There was the equivalent of a concierge desk where a long and slow-moving line had formed. *Long* because of the six-foot distancing rules. *Slow* because what line didn't move at a snail's pace in today's pandemic world? I tilted my head back, resting it on the top of the chair, and looked up at the ceiling, closing my eyes for a moment.

A familiar sound unexpectedly wafted into my ears. A deep, gregarious laugh that hadn't warmed my heart in years. And there was another voice I recognized but couldn't quite place. The loudness of their discussion escalated, and I was drawn to it, like to a congregation of people at a party having the most fun.

I got up from my chair and followed the sounds around a small partition to a table where two men sat comfortably, waving their hands in the air to emphasize conversational points over a small collection of beer bottles and steins. Two men I couldn't be happier to see. Under my mask, a cheek to cheek smile cemented itself in place.

The man with the deep laugh was facing me and carrying on a steady, maskless conversation. He had a dark complexion and long Rastafarian type flaming red dreadlocks tied back in a loose tail, a diamond stud in his right ear, and large tattoos on both bare forearms partially covered by the rolled-up sleeves of a black dress shirt – upon which, if you looked close enough, you could see a pattern of tiny, white skulls and crossbones. His eyes diverted from his partner to fix directly on mine, and the words coming out of his mouth froze in mid-air. He stood from his chair and in that baritone voice with an overdone, alcohol fueled, Jamaican accent said, "Dr. Mark Spencer, *mon*. Is that you?"

"Dr. Rufus Leandro," I replied, "it most certainly is."

***

"Come, come. Sit with us, my friend, and tell me of your adventures," Rufus exclaimed jubilantly as he pulled a chair out. "And let me introduce you to my new friend, Mr. –"

"– Mr. Charlie Treemont," I beamed.

"You know each –" A look of surprise overtook Rufus' face.

"– Ahh, *you* are the doctor that Chuck was just telling me about, going to England with the dying father. The one he met on the plane, full of bountiful ideas. I should have guessed."

"That would be me," I sighed, sitting down heavily, and dropping my backpack on the floor next to my chair. I hesitantly removed my mask and placed it in my pocket. It was a strange thing. An hour ago, I was sitting near Charlie on the plane and the concept of wearing a mask was of utmost importance, like my life depended on it. Now, as we gathered around this table to socialize, the risks versus benefits of wearing a mask somehow altered. The benefits of conversation and camaraderie suddenly seemed to outweigh the small risks of getting Covid. It was completely illogical and very human.

"I'm so excited to see you, my friend," Rufus said, "although, perhaps, under more pleasant circumstances would be better. What brings you to La Belle Province and what's this about your father?"

"*That*, is a long and complicated story."

"Well, in these slow times of Covid, a long story is righteously what I need to hear."

With a flick of his fingers, Rufus had a beer sitting in front of me, and I delivered my saga to the best of my abilities. You see, Rufus was a storyteller, and any story worth telling to Rufus must be told as if, at the end of every sentence, a magical being might erupt from the middle of the table and do an Irish Jig right then and there. He hung on my every word, only interrupting at times to throw his hands in the air and then slap the table in amazement, causing our drinks to teeter, but never spill.

Of course, this story led backwards to my disastrous trip south to save Sarah in March, when I caught Covid. He absorbed it all, as if he'd never heard anything more fascinating in his entire life. Charlie, meanwhile, listened patiently, shaking his head, and nodding.

"Ahh, my friend," Rufus said, when he was finally up to speed, "it is very fortunate that you have run into me."

"On that note," I said, "a big thank you to Chuck for giving me his Gold Lounge voucher."

"My pleasure, Doc. Things always work out for a reason, right?"

Sometimes, I thought. I had no idea what to do about getting to London at the moment. In my experience, it was always best to let my subconscious handle the unsolvable problems. And right now, getting to London was unsolvable. A few drinks with new and old friends was exactly what I needed.

"So, Doc," Charlie asked, "how do you and Rufus know each other?"

Rufus and I exchanged glances and smiled. Strangely, we had first met under similar circumstances, many years ago. At the time, we were both on the medical school interview circuit trying to fulfill our dreams. We met in a bar in this very airport, both of us killing time, waiting for our flights.

"Medical school, class of '01, at McGill," I said.

"What? Rufus? You're a medical doctor? I had no idea. I thought you were a businessman or investor."

"Well, I am all those things, but I have not practiced medicine for many years."

In the early days of his medical career, Rufus had written a novel which went to number one on the New York Times bestseller list. He made a small fortune from this book which he then invested in gold stocks at exactly the right time. More importantly, he sold at the right time. Suddenly, he was a very wealthy man who never had to work again. He retired from medicine shortly thereafter in favor of world travel and angel investing, which I presumed was why Charlie, the mask salesman, was here. This reminded me, "Guys, I'm assuming you're here conducting business. I hope I haven't interrupted anything?"

"No problem, Doc," Charlie said. "We had just finished up when you arrived. Meet my new silent partner in CustoMask Inc." He waved his hand at Rufus, who bowed his head and said, "Yes. Chuck is very convincing. And if custom designed masks make even one more person wear them, then we are doing good things for the world. Right?" He looked to me for confirmation.

"Absolutely," I said. "As long as they're the right masks with scientifically proven efficacy." I winked at Charlie, and he smiled.

"You got it, Doc. Safety first. Then fashion." Charlie checked his phone. "Looks like my flight is on time. Gentlemen, it was a pleasure sharing some fine ale with you. Rufus, I'll send some documents your way. Doc, it was great running into you again and, as I said, if you have any more brilliant ideas, please contact me."

Charlie exchanged knuckles with both of us and then left the lounge on the run.

Sadly, that was the last time I would ever speak with Charlie Treemont.

*****

A different waitress wandered over, asking if we wanted more beverages. She was wearing one of those new, clear plastic face masks that was molded to fit her facial contours with plastic loops around her ears. Having had several rounds already, we declined.

"What do you think of her mask?" Rufus asked. "It would have been good if Chuck were here to see it. He was talking about a new clear mask that would allow people to see each other's faces. 'Face Sharing Masks,' I think he called them."

I chuckled to myself. Sometimes a little idea could go a long way.

I'd read about these new plastic masks, worn and endorsed by celebrities of all kind. They made no sense whatsoever to me since there was no filtration process, no minimum three layers of material to trap infectious organisms. Effectively the wearer was simply breathing around the edges of the mask, like a shield. It was the worst of all worlds, since neither the wearer nor the people around the wearer were really protected.

"They're an interesting concept, Rufus, and they solve some problems for people who are hearing impaired for lip reading, but they ultimately provide very little protection as masks. I wouldn't recommend them for your new company."

"Yes, but I like seeing the pretty faces again." He released a long sigh. "It's very hard to meet people now, Mark, with Covid. And when you do, you can't really see them. You can't really tell if you're attracted to them."

"Still single, Rufus?"

"Alas, it is so, *mon*." He pushed a long dreadlock of red hair that had come free back behind his ear. "I'm beginning to think there is no right woman for a man like me. You are very lucky to be married, Mark, in times like these. Very lucky."

I certainly couldn't argue with that statement. Sarah was the greatest thing that had ever happened to me. "Don't worry. There's someone out there for you. You just have to find them."

"Easier said than done, my friend."

The waitress passed by us again heading to another table. Rufus followed her with his eyes. And then continued, "You're sure that mask is no good?"

"Definitely not."

"I trust your medical savvy, *mon*. Are you sure you don't want to join our little company? Think of the good you could do for the Covid pandemic and any future pandemics. Not to mention making a few dollars on the side."

"Let me sort out this trip to England first and then I'll talk it over with Sarah. Okay?"

"Excellent."

"Mark, I've been meaning to ask," Rufus continued, "I know it's important for you to see your dad and set things right between you, but is this potential cure so important? I mean, we are probably months away from having a vaccine. Won't that make your cure obsolete, if it even exists?"

That was a good question and one that I'd researched extensively before leaving home.

"To be honest, Rufus, I'm not sure. Think of all the obstacles that have to be overcome for a vaccine to be effective worldwide. To begin with, this is a *novel* type of virus, which has never really been seen before. This means a completely new vaccine has to be developed and manufactured almost from scratch, requiring a colossal technological effort. The early studies coming out on the mRNA vaccines are promising in terms of effectiveness, but there are still hundreds of unanswered questions, like: if it provides effective immunity, how long will that immunity last for? If it works, will it prevent asymptomatic transmission to those who don't have, or can't have, the vaccine? Will it be of any use for a second or third strain of SARS-CoV-2? Will there be short term side effects? How about long term, completely unexpected side effects? Will it work in kids? Pregnant women? The list goes on and on …

"And even if a perfect vaccine is developed in a reasonable amount of time, there's the matter of distribution, getting it to everyone – in the entire world! – to create the necessary herd immunity.

"And then even if you could get it to everyone who wanted it, the fact is: not everyone wants it. There's this whole concept of 'vaccine hesitancy,' the idea that many people would delay or refuse to take a vaccine even if it was available."

"Ahh, the anti-vaxxers." Rufus interrupted, nodding his head.

"Not really. Pure anti-vaxxers, who would not accept a vaccine under any circumstances and for whatever personal reasons, actually represent a relatively small percentage. A recent Pew Research Center poll done in September showed that only 51% 'probably' or 'would' take the vaccine if it were available at that time. That's not very high and certainly not high enough to stop the spread of COVID-19.

"So, you have to make a brand new vaccine, somehow distribute it to everyone, and then convince enough people to take it to create herd immunity to protect those who can't or won't take it. Can that be done? I'm not so sure, and I'm not convinced anyone can be sure."

"You need to have patience, my friend." Rufus answered. "All of these questions will be answered in time."

"But how much time?" I countered. "And how many people will die in the interim? People like my father."

"I hear your pain, *mon*. This has become a very emotional quest for you."

"No. I disagree. This is pure logic. Anyone in my shoes would do the same. They would have to …."

"My friend, you have always been a dreamer of grand adventures. I think you overestimate the average person's courage, and you underestimate the power of your emotions."

"Rufus, if you were in my shoes, wouldn't you do everything you could to obtain a possible cure? Something in case the vaccine doesn't work, or at least something to augment the treatment armamentarium, if the vaccine does work?"

He smiled and shrugged his shoulders. "Fortunately, you and I have a different shoe size."

Rufus poured me a full glass of beer, smiled, and said, "After that longwinded monologue, you must be parched."

He was right. Not about being parched, but about my emotions. They were playing a bigger role in this quest than I cared to admit. I gulped a healthy portion of beer and began to consider this, however, it all seemed academic now that my journey had hit an insurmountable wall.

Rufus suddenly asked, "Say, do you have a place to stay, my friend? Since your flight home isn't leaving until tomorrow."

"Not yet. You and Chuck were my first stop after I learned my flight was cancelled." I was swirling my Bière Maudites and was feeling a little buzzed. I really didn't feel like going anywhere.

"Then, you must stay with me. I have many extra rooms. And we can order in dinner tonight from your favorite, Garde Manger."

I smiled; Rufus still remembered my favorite restaurant in Old Montreal. My stomach grumbled, and I realized I never did get that Montreal smoked meat sandwich I ordered at my other table. "Sounds delish. Still have that mansion in Westmount?"

"Yes. I love my house."

There were some perks to having a wealthy friend. "Sure. I'd love to. Let me call Sarah and let her know my plans."

"Yes. And tell your beautiful wife I may have an idea to get you to London."

***

"Okay. I think you've dragged this out long enough, Rufus. What's this idea you have?"

A wonderful seafood platter had been delivered an hour earlier. We were seated in Rufus' extravagant dining room that could easily fit twenty guests, just the two of us sipping a well-aged, pricey, Napa Valley boutique wine called Screaming Eagle that he'd brought up from his cellar.

"Patience, *mon*." He was slurring a little. "I still be putting the final touches on things."

Rufus had always been an amazing friend and although we'd drifted apart over the last five years as he travelled the world – in search of what? Adventure? Love?? – our friendship bonds had been welded over many a brew during the terrors of medical school and would not easily be broken. His fortunes really hadn't changed him that much, except in smaller ways. One of his quirkier things, now that he had money, was that he liked to surprise his friends, at any cost. This could be endearing, but sometimes, as with right now, it could be very frustrating.

"Look, Rufus. I need to tell my mother something, anything." I stood from my seat and placed both hands on the table, looking directly at Rufus. I envisioned a steady flow of steam emanating from my ears. "You know my situation. Time is crucial."

"Ahh, your father is a different man," Rufus replied, taking a long sip from his wine glass. "Very smart. And a top microbiologist and virologist. If anyone could develop a cure, it would be him. We will get you to London."

I sat down. "How could you possibly get me to London? The borders are closed. Only planes carrying

British citizens are allowed. It's not like we can hop in a car and drive there. I know cash is king, but in this case even your Scrooge vault of money won't help."

I looked at Rufus, who was leaning back on his chair's two rear legs, his chin tucked in, his eyes twinkling, and a thin mischievous smile parked on his face.

"Mark, you have *no* plan at this point. At dawn tomorrow morning, I will show you *my plan* and not a minute sooner. Now, we get some rest."

***

I remember ...

There was this Elm tree at the edge of a forest ten minutes from my house. It towered over every other tree, and townspeople said it was over two hundred years old. One of the very few elms left alive after Dutch elm disease scourged the British countryside in the 1960's and 70's. I was twelve and imagined that the view of our little town of Netley from the top would be mesmerizing. I had saved my allowance and purchased a small Kodak Ektralite camera. My dad loved photographs. He respected the truthfulness of a photo. A photograph (back then) didn't purposefully lie, it was naked reality. I wanted to take a panoramic photograph of Netley from the sky. The top of the Elm was as close as I could get.

The Elm had perfect branches designed by mother nature as a step ladder to the sky for kids. Unfortunately, they only started at the halfway point, a good thirty feet above the ground. Next to the Elm, was an equally impressive oak, though not nearly as tall. My plan was to climb the oak and shimmy out along a large branch that reached over to the Elm, where its perfect climbing branches awaited. I assembled a backpack filled with rope, a hammer, nails to use as pitons, a grappling hook that I found in our shed, a heavy belt, and a pair of gloves.

It was a great plan, until my rope snapped.

This was my sixth week in skeletal traction for a badly broken femur. The doctors said I was very lucky and could've easily broken every other part of my body including my neck. After six weeks in bed with a steel traction pin through the end of my femur, I didn't feel very lucky. There was no pain to speak of anymore, just boredom.

My mother piled a stack of worksheets on my hospital table. "And this is from Mrs. Addington. She was very impressed. One hundred percent on your algebra quiz."

"Great," I said. "I suppose she wants to give me extra assignments now?"

Another stack landed on my table and my mother grinned.

"Any chance Dad's coming by to see me? I've only been here six weeks and he still hasn't visited." My voice dripped acid.

"Your dad's very busy at work. I've only seen him a little bit myself. He tells me he's on the verge of —"

"Yeah, yeah, I know. Another breakthrough. I've heard it a million times."

"He asks about you all the time, and he phones the doctors for progress reports daily."

"Great. Just wonderful ...."

"Mark, I know it's hard, but you only have two more weeks in the hospital and then you'll be home."

Sure, in a hip spica cast from my toes to my armpits for another six weeks.

I turned my head away to look out the window. I was in a four-kid ward and only recently got moved to a highly coveted spot with a view. Ironically, in the far distance across a field, I could now see my Elm tree looming portentously over Netley. On the windowsill was my copy of Tolkien's *The Lord of the Rings* and I was reminded of the giant Ent character, Treebeard. If my Elm was Treebeard, he would have been laughing down at me in a wise, booming voice, saying, "You dare?" as I lay in broken pieces at the base of his trunk.

"Your father sent you something …"

I looked back at my mother as she withdrew a large box from a brown paper bag she was carrying. She carefully moved the paperwork off my table and placed the box directly in front of me.

It was a model ship kit of the HMS *Victory*.

"Your father thought this would keep you very busy and help you pass the time."

I released a muted, lengthy groan. *He has no time to visit me, but he has time to go to a hobby shop? Bet my mother bought it, anyway.*

"Mark, I have to go, but I'll be back tomorrow around the same time. Okay? Do you need anything?"

I shook my head from side to side and then my mother departed.

Two more bloody weeks, I thought.

I lifted the box a few inches off the table and dropped it, listening to all the pieces rattle around. I did this repeatedly from greater and greater heights feeling a little volcano of hate erupt deep in my gut. I dropped it one last time from as high as my arms would reach and then stared at it for a moment before whacking it off the table and into the window. It fell to the floor and broke apart, sending pieces all over, laying there, like a half-open treasure chest of broken promises.

Dads are supposed to build the models with their kids.

My nurse delivered a lunch tray promptly at noon. Her name was Susan. She was pretty, and I was awkward. She noticed the model ship box disaster on the floor.

"Drop something?"

"Sort of," I squeaked.

She gathered all the stray pieces and put them back in the box. "Where do you want it?"

I eyed the trash can next to my side dresser, scrunched my eyes closed and clenched my teeth in deep thought. I wanted to build that ship.

Damn him.

I stretched both hands out acceptingly towards Susan.

12 Days Earlier

November 7th, 2020

"Rufus! Are you completely out of your fucking mind? You want to sail to England? On a fucking sailboat? My eyes were explosively wide, like two grenades.

"Hear me out, Mark." He had both hands up, palms facing me, like he was protecting himself. "I was going to winter in Greece, anyway. I wasn't planning to leave until next week, but I moved up the timetable. I'll make a small detour and drop you off at Southampton before heading south. From the marina in Southampton, you can catch a cab to your parent's place. See? Easy peasy, *mon*?"

"You're insane. Cross the Atlantic Ocean in November? It will be freezing, and it will take a month. I needed to be there today."

Rufus had dropped his "surprise bomb" a moment earlier, when we arrived at the Yacht Club in the Bassin de L'Horloge of Old Montreal, and he had escorted me through locked gates and across a dock to stand in front of a ginormous, beautiful sailboat – the *Rumrunner*. It was twice as long as any other boat in the marina and commanded its own private jetty complete with personalized gangway. The dawn sun had just crested the horizon casting lengthy shadows from the dozen or so other sailboats that still remained in the marina, not yet pulled out to be stored and winterized.

"Don't be a li'l baby, *mon*. You can't be there today, or tomorrow. I checked the news before we left this morning and they're predicting the borders will be closed for months. The *Rumrunner* is your only chance."

"But that is *so* crazy and will take forever." I simply couldn't wrap my mind around this "surprise" plan.

"I've crossed three times, *by myself*," Rufus said. If anyone else had claimed this it would have been boasting, but for Rufus, it was just fact. It was what he did. "I've made it in sixteen days, but at this time of year, with the westerly winds and two people, I think we can do it in twelve days, pushing hard."

"Fuuuck," was all I could say. "I can't believe this is your great plan."

It was insane, but then again, so was crossing ice encrusted shipping lanes by kayak last March.

Rufus knew I was a sucker for a good adventure. *I* knew I was a sucker for good adventure, or even a *bad* one. I just couldn't learn.

I dropped my pack onto the dock, hard, and took a half dozen steps back from the *Rumrunner* such that I was standing on the edge of the dock taking in the whole ship in one sweeping view. She *was* magnificent: A sixty-foot ketch with a main and mizzenmast; she had teak railings that were already gleaming in the early light; brass fittings that winked morning sunrays in every direction; a large cockpit just in front of the rear mizzenmast that held a huge ships wheel, its spokes weaved with whipping twine for better grip. Rufus had gushed extensively about acquiring this vessel five years ago, before his world travels. It was apparently one of the fastest vessels of its kind. Rufus would joke that it could make the Kessel Run faster than the Millennium Falcon. It had even been featured in several big budget Hollywood movies, including the modern version of The Great Gatsby with DiCaprio.

"I have the finest food and wine onboard, enough to last two people a month, my friend." Rufus continued to lay the bait.

"Twelve days?" I said, taking a big breath and looking up at the sky for some divine sign.

"If we are good. And a bit lucky. Yes. Twelve days."

It felt like the devil was perched on one shoulder and an angel on the other. But which one was Rufus?

I pulled out my phone and started playing with it, flipping it over and over, like a coin toss. Still debating, thinking. What choice did I really have? A dying father. A possible cure for Covid. "I'll have to check with Sarah, and I guarantee you she won't like it. Not one bit."

Rufus reached out and slowly grabbed the phone from my hand. He stepped to the edge of the *Rumrunner* and gently tossed it underhand into a netting inside the cockpit.

"It's too early to call. You'll wake the beautiful lady, and she'll be cranky. Call her when we're underway."

"But –"

"No buts, Mark. Get onboard, we're burning daylight. This will be your greatest adventure yet, my friend."

And, quite possibly, my final adventure.

***

The *Rumrunner* pulled away from the dock, out of the mouth of the Bassin de l'Horloge and into the Saint Lawrence River with her diesel engine puffing small dark clouds from her rear exhaust. Captain Rufus was at the wheel, deftly manoeuvring the craft around markers with a focus that rivaled the rising sun in intensity, and a smile that belayed his natural love for the sea. After stowing all of the lines, I stood at the bow and did a slow 360 degree turn, admiring memorable surroundings that I hadn't seen in many years.

Directly on my starboard, or right side, casting a tall strip of darkness across the stern, was the clock tower, or Tour de l'Horloge as it was known locally. Completed in 1921, after two years of construction, it honored Canadian sailors who died in both World Wars. I remembered racing Rufus up the 192 steps to the top on graduation day, our stomachs full of the same seafood platter we'd had last evening.

Further on the right, past the clock tower and across the river, sat Île Sainte Hélène, home of the amusement park La Ronde that once laid claim to the world's longest wooden roller coaster. Rufus and I still held a McGill record for most consecutive rides – or so we'd like to believe.

Off the stern, or back of the ship, to the south, was the newest addition to the waterfront: the Montreal Observation Wheel. Much like the London Eye, this giant Ferris wheel, erected in 2017, gave a panoramic view of the city and waterways. Sarah and I had planned to come back to Montreal this past summer and spend some time on the waterfront taking in the sights. Despite Sarah's fear of heights, I'd hoped to get her on the Wheel. I wondered when we would ever be able to come back. The latest projections for the pandemic were now extending into 2023. Our baby would be three years old and know nothing but a world in a constant state of pandemic malaise. I released a long sigh of dismay and turned 180 degrees to face forward, to the north, *to the future*. Faint rays of sunlight gleamed off of the Jacques-Cartier Bridge which spanned a rapidly flowing Saint Lawrence River. The plan was to follow this river all the way north, past Québec City, and into the Gulf of Saint Lawrence. All of this would be under motor, with refueling stops along the way, and our last stop being St. John's, Newfoundland, before hitting open water. Sarah had always talked about visiting Newfoundland –

A vibrating phone suddenly smothered my daydreams.

Shit, Sarah.

***

"Rufus, is there a place I can charge my phone?"

"At the navigation table down below, there's an outlet."

"The generator won't fry it or anything?"

Rufus laughed. "This the queen of boats, *mon.* It don't fry anything except a good steak and eggs. Didn't you charge it last night at my house?"

"I did, but it apparently has a battery problem. Supposedly fixed before I left, but …"

Rufus nodded his head. "Your conversation with Sarah, I could hear parts of it, even all the way back here. It didn't go well."

"Hmm, you could definitely say that." I sagged down into the cockpit on a bench across from Rufus and suddenly felt the chill of a three-thousand-mile journey pass through me. I zipped my parka up to my neck and pulled my tuque down a little further.

"She's pissed?"

"Oh, I'd say she's well beyond pissed. She's at some level of anger I've never seen before. Let's see, she used words like asshole, idiot, stupid, stupid idiot, betrayal. That last one really hurt.

"And then short snappers like: How could you? What are you thinking? What about your job? It's Rufus, for God's sake! You're not a sailor!

"And then some nasty sentences like: Do you have a death wish? If you don't die on your stupid adventure, I'll kill you. Don't you care about your unborn child? Don't you care about me?"

Rufus laughed. "You're a funny man, Mark. When you talk fast a hint of your old British accent gets sprinkled into your words."

"Well, I'm glad you think it's funny because I bloody well don't."

He adjusted the throttle and helm as we came around a red channel marker and then continued. "Don't worry, *mon*. The pretty lady will come around. I know she will."

"Well, you didn't fare so well in the conversation either. I believe there are now cockroaches that she holds in higher esteem than you."

Another deep laugh escaped his belly. "Well, my friend, cockroaches will still be here when the earth turns to dust. That's a compliment."

"Fairly certain she didn't intend it as one. And, to top it all off, my stupid phone died mid conversation."

"Probably a good thing and meant to be. Give her time to think about it. I tell you, she'll come around."

I wasn't so sure.

***

I remember ...

It was the end of my third week in Montreal. I was 13 and had just started classes at Bishop's College, a boarding school. My parents had decided that a few years in Montreal was just the thing I needed to meet other kids and keep me out of trouble. The incident with the Elm tree had been a deciding factor. They also felt it would be a good steppingstone towards getting me into McGill University. My dad had been highly impressed with the school following his three-year sabbatical.

"How are you, Mark. Are they treating you well?" My dad asked. He sounded distant, like he was at the office on his computer. It was the first time he'd contacted me since I moved to Canada. My mum called me every other day.

"Pretty good, I guess," I replied. "You know, they fingerprinted me again the minute I arrived. Said the original set we sent from home with the application was smudged, or something."

"Is that right? Good," my father said. "Can't ever take security too lightly, now, can we?"

"I guess," I replied, not entirely convinced.

A spell of dead air passed. "I've been here three weeks now. You haven't called."

"Has it been three weeks already? My goodness the time flies. Work is terribly busy." I wondered if the real reason I was sent to boarding school wasn't to get me out of my dad's hair. Rid him of his obligation to spend time with me. Rid him of any guilt he might have for not being there.

"How are you getting along with your classmates?"

"Well, they're making fun of me." I replied.

"Really? In what way?" His voice suddenly had inflection. I had his attention.

"Apparently, I have an accent. They walk around the halls doing lousy imitations of me. *Blimey,*

Mark. Top of the morning, Mark. Cheerio, Mark. Bloody hell, Mark. I can't stand it!"

"Then perhaps you should eliminate your accent."

"Eliminate my accent?"

It turned out, I was facile with languages. Eight months later, when I returned home for the summer, my accent was gone. My mother was horrified, and my father simply smiled.

10 Days Earlier

November 9th, 2020

Day 3 at Sea

After three days at sea under motor, with one short fueling stop yesterday in Québec City, we were approaching the estuary, the point where fresh water transitioned to salt as the Great Lakes mixed with the Atlantic Ocean. Since we were sailing with the current, the *Rumrunner* was making excellent headway at more than ten knots.

We settled into the rhythm of sea life very quickly. During the day, Rufus gave me a crash course on every detail of the *Rumrunner* from engine mechanics and steering mechanism to the various sails and all the lines and ropes that controlled them. The *Rumrunner* ran comfortably in the navigation channels, chugging along with minimal effort even with the throttle almost wide open. Displacing 32.5 tonnes, it left a huge wake at these speeds, the kind that you could surf on. Occasionally, as we passed through narrower channels where cottages dotted the coastline, we had to drop our speed to prevent the *Rumrunner*'s wake from damaging docks and other vessels tied up alongside. Besides that, we were pushing full speed ahead at all times. Rufus assured me that the 115 HP diesel engine had recently been rebuilt and could handle it with ease.

Overnight, we took turns at the helm in four-hour shifts, much as you would on a warship, working three watches of four hours from 8 PM until 8 AM. As an ER physician, I was used to working evening shifts, although, typically, I would be able to catch up on sleep at home the following day. This was not the case on the *Rumrunner*, where there was work to be done during daylight hours: cooking, cleaning, maintenance, etc. The overall routine reminded me of residency and taking in-house call over long periods. Sleep deprivation slowly and steadily creeping into your whole being, fogging your mind, and zapping the strength from your muscles. I knew I would get used to it eventually, as I had in the past. Still, the adaptation period was challenging.

Rufus, on the other hand, was truly in his realm, like a surgeon in an operating room or fireman on his truck. Something about being the captain of the ship transcended his need for sleep. Like a chameleon, he seemed to have instantly adapted to his environment. Not infrequently, I would catch him in a quick catnap that appeared to rejuvenate his mind and body, as if he'd had a full night's sleep.

From a conversation perspective, we had fully caught up by this point and had made that transition to creating new memories that was so important to maintaining a friendship. You could only relive the past so many times before it became stale. Rufus really had sailed the world over the past five years and had lived more adventure during that time than I ever would in my whole life. Contrary to Sarah's opinion, I was just a guppy in the sea of adventure seekers. Rufus, on the other hand, was the Antarctic Blue Whale. If he hadn't experienced it, it probably wasn't worth experiencing. I'll admit, I was a little jealous initially, but I was quick to realize that he carried a subtle aura of loneliness about him, like he was permanently weighed down with a heavy winter coat that was just a shade too large. I had a feeling he would give all of this up in an instant, if the right woman came along.

The only other vessels on the water were freighters hauling their massive loads up and down the river to faraway destinations. Sometimes, we would pass a thousand-footer and ride in her wake, memories of my kayak adventure in March resurfacing and once again sending a shiver up my spine. Rufus had an App on his phone that identified the vessels based on a picture scan, much like scanning a barcode. The App also provided real time information. We passed the hours by guessing: Where they were originating from? Where they were going? What they were carrying? And a hundred other details. It began as a betting game that I quickly abandoned once I realized the futility of betting against a man with unlimited funds and a life lived largely on the water for the past five years.

I spoke with Sarah, or attempted to, several times a day. As of this morning, she seemed to have come to terms with the next part of my journey, ultimately deciding that she didn't want me to die while she was still pissed at me. Not exactly reassuring.

I also contacted my mother daily, getting updates. My father was still ventilated in the ICU and holding his own. My mother had seen the news of the border closures and realized there was no other way for me to come home. Initially, she wasn't thrilled about my method of transportation and tried to talk me out of it, but, by the second day, she had already absorbed it as a simple fact of life.

"Mark is taking a sailboat home with his old schoolmate, Rufus, across the Atlantic Ocean to see his sick father. He'll be here in a few weeks." I loved that about my mother, her pragmatic nature, and her ability to adapt to any situation with minimal fuss.

We passed the last of the season's cruise ships soaking up sites like the magnificent Chateau Frontenac in Québec City, the quaint and colorful Harrington Harbour fishing village, Tadoussac – one of the oldest European settlements in Canada, and the Saguenay Fjord – an ideal whale watching environment where, even without the warmth of the sun, you were sure to find passengers hanging off of the ship railings trying to catch the slap of a tail or the spray of a blow spout.

It was late afternoon, and we both sat in the cockpit, lulled by the steady thrum of the engine. I noticed the water changing color to a deeper blue and the current increasing in speed, propelling us even faster.

"The estuary?" I asked.

"Oh, yes, *mon*. Beautiful, isn't it?"

The setting sun was low over our left shoulders. It reflected off the turbulent emerald colored mixture of salt and fresh water on our port side and cast long, infinite shadows of the *Rumrunner* off our starboard side. The swirling waters blended into one, as if thrown together in a baker's mixing bowl.

"How fast is the current here?"

"Very, very fast. Almost eight knots."

We passed a green marker that was lying at a 45-degree angle as its anchor pulled against the rapidly flowing water.

"How fast is the *Rumrunner* going?"

Rufus leaned his head to the side to better visualize the speedometer on his console. He let out a whoop. "Fifteen knots!"

He looked at me and then jammed the throttle all the way forward, smiling broadly as he yelled over the full speed thunder of the engine, "Let's see if the *Rumrunner* will plane."

Because of the *Rumrunner*'s displacement weight this was an impossibility, and he knew it. The engine coughed a little as it hit maximum RPMs.

"Rufus, you're crazy!"

"My friend, the *Rumrunner* and I will get you to England in time to see your father alive and maybe to save the world, or … we will die trying."

These words would prove unnervingly prophetic.

9 Days Earlier

November 10th, 2020

Day 4 at Sea

With dawn of our fourth day at sea, we began to feel the steady push of the westerlies that would eventually carry us across the Atlantic Ocean. Gaspé was somewhere far in the distance off our starboard side, and Anticosti Island was a distant speck off our port side. I took the helm, and Rufus, looking a dozen years younger and moving with chimp-like acrobatic comfort, began raising, one by one, all five sails that the *Rumrunner* had to offer. The forward sails billowed and bucked as Rufus adjusted the sheets until each sail captured its fair share of forward propulsion, and the

Rumrunner gradually increased its speed until the wake behind us looked like a giant rooster tail.

At first, the *Rumrunner* vibrated erratically, looking for equilibrium between the great winds off the stern and the deep, dark waves off the bow. And then Rufus tweaked a line here and a line there, adjusted the position of the boom on the mizzenmast and then the main and, finally, pulled in on the boom vang. Suddenly, ship, wind, and ocean coalesced into this magical thing of sublime perfection. I imagined at that moment that there were no limits to what speeds we could achieve, and reaching England, for the first time, seemed real and only moments away.

Rufus let out a loud, "Wahoo," as the spray from a lively wave covered him, and I answered with an even louder one. I had never felt this close to source, so in tune with the world. A perfect synchronicity of man, object, and nature.

"Mark," Rufus yelled through the wind, "how fast?"

The orange fiery ball had now crested the horizon casting a blinding reflection at our backs and onto the navigation panel. I bent my head and blocked the light with my gloved hand. My eyes opened wide as I registered the speed. *Unbelievable*. I yelled back, "Seventeen knots, Rufus. Seventeen freakin' knots." Faster than our maximum motor speed.

Rufus launched an ear to ear smile and then let out another, "Wahoo."

At this speed, we would be there in five days.

"Look," Rufus yelled excitedly, pointing to something in the water not far off our starboard side.

I engaged the autopilot, grabbed a pair of binoculars, and then stood on my seat. I scanned the direction where Rufus was pointing. At first, there was nothing but rolling waves topped by white caps. Then, a glistening white mass crested the top of a larger wave not a hundred meters from the *Rumrunner,* followed by "V" shaped tail flukes that seemed to freeze momentarily in space before crashing down hard and sending a circle of white spray high into the air.

"Beluga," Rufus shouted as he stepped down into the cockpit. "Very rare."

I had never seen anything like it. It was magnificent.

"Now, you are happy, my friend?" Rufus put his arm over my shoulder and gave me a squeeze.

I nodded. I might only have been happier once in my life.

***

I remember ...

"He said he'd be here."

"My friend, you're getting married in five minutes. Look around you. Everyone is here and waiting."

Out of the corner of my eye, I scanned the nave. Rufus was right. All of our family and friends were sitting and ready for the ceremony to begin. Sarah and her father were cloistered behind the two large entry doors waiting for the first notes. My mum was in the front row on the groom's side, an empty seat next to her. She had flown by herself from England to Montreal three days earlier. My father was to arrive this morning.

"Can we stall a little?" I asked.

"I'll check." Rufus climbed the alter and pulled the minister aside. I could hear them whispering. He quickly returned, and said, "Sorry. The minister says he has another wedding next hour. If the bride and groom are here the ceremony must go on."

One of the great entrance doors opened and an usher, a favorite cousin on Sarah's side, dressed in a tuxedo, walked quickly down the aisle carrying an envelope. He delivered it directly to my mother. I watched her open and read it. The look on her face revealed exactly what I expected. She looked up, caught my eye, and waved me over.

"I'm sorry, Mark. Your father can't make your wedding. He was late getting away from work and missed his flight this morning." She looked at me with doleful eyes, asking forgiveness for the man she loved.

She read the note once more. "He says he'll pay for everything."

I looked up at the ceiling vault and smiled sardonically. I had become an expert at accepting disappointment. "Mum, I can pay for my own wedding."

I hesitated for just a second before whispering something that was long overdue, "To hell with him."

I turned and gave Rufus the thumbs up. Rufus in turn waved to the organ player who was sitting high up in the balcony at the back of the church.

I took my place at the altar with Rufus at my side. I nodded to the minister and then inhaled deeply to steady myself. The sounds of Wagner's Bridal Chorus reverberated throughout the church, and my legs instantly turned to mush. The doors at the back of the church opened wide as the world around me disappeared and the ethereal vision that was my wife-to-be floated down the aisle and took my breath away.

To hell with my father.

We have not spoken since.

8 Days Earlier

November 11th, 2020

Day 5 at Sea

"What do you mean there's no diesel fuel, Rufus?" I was standing mid deck, just behind the mainmast, facing the fueling jetty we had tied up to thirty minutes earlier. Rufus was on the jetty and had just come back from a heated discussion with the fuel station attendant. His mask was hanging off of one ear lobe and his shoulders sagged. As we passed the southern tip of Newfoundland, the winds had continued to howl in perfect harmony with the *Rumrunner*, keeping our speeds steady. It was a difficult decision to drop the sails and head into the Port of St. John's. Part of me felt like we would never see winds like that again and that we were giving up something special. Rufus was adamant that we had little chance of completing our journey with only a quarter tank of diesel fuel. The winds were bound to lag at some point necessitating the motor. Not to mention the generator and the need to navigate the English Channel when we got there. St. John's was the last gas for over 2000 nautical miles.

"That's what the man said. No diesel fuel in Newfoundland because of Covid and a supply problem."

"He said there's no diesel fuel *anywhere* in Newfoundland?"

"Nowhere here."

"You're sure you understood him, with his Newfie accent, and all?"

"Yes, *mon*. I spent a couple of months here in St. John's a few years ago, doing some work on the *Rumrunner*. I even picked up the accent for a while …, b'y." Rufus grinned just a little as he said this last part.

I could barely imagine what a Jamaican/Newfie accent would sound like. "Okay, so what now? We have a quarter tank of fuel. How long could we motor with that if we had to?"

"Depends how fast. Maybe a full day."

"So, maybe 24 hours of motor time, leaving a little in the tank for docking purposes when we get there."

Rufus nodded hesitantly. He had a strange, unfathomable look on his face. Almost deflated, like someone had sucked all the joy from his body. Resignation? *Is he giving up?*

He replied in a low, gravelly voice, "Give or take." There was a long pause and his head hung low as he fidgeted from side to side before kicking a small pebble off the dock and into the water at the edge of the *Rumrunner*. He looked up towards me but didn't make eye contact. "Maybe this is a sign. Maybe it is meant to be that we go no further."

Meant to be. I shook my head; I hated those three words. If I had truly accepted every obstacle that I had encountered on this journey as a sign of things that were *meant to be*, then I would have never left home. We were taught in medical school and in residency to *achieve our goals at all and any cost*: get that IV in, track down the missing blood test, negotiate to have the CT head done now and not tomorrow, convince the stubborn old man to take his pills, persuade the young mother that her child needs an operation to survive. *Save the patient, no matter what.*

We were chosen for these qualities to be doctors. And maybe this was ancient thinking and times had changed to allow for more leeway and alternate paths to solve a problem. Accepting that sometimes things *were* meant to be and that if you allowed yourself to be blocked, other paths would open up. Better paths. Easier paths. The problem was that at my core, because of my training, it was my instinct to bulldoze through to the end point I had set out to achieve. Perhaps, with time and effort, I could change. But not today. The only things that were *meant to be* today were what I made of them. There was no way I could turn back.

"We can do this, Rufus. Can't we? We can make it there with a quarter tank?"

Rufus left the question hanging and slowly boarded the *Rumrunner* carrying a brown bag in his right hand. He sat on a bench in the cockpit and waved me over to the seat across from him. He looked incredibly pensive as he opened the bag and delivered a bottle of some sort.

"Have you had the local Screech before?"

"Maybe," I replied.

"Not like this one. They make it in a shed behind the ice cream shop over there." He pointed his finger in the direction of the small row of multicolored buildings he had briefly visited before coming back from his recon mission. "It burns of tobacco and old leather. The best."

He unfolded the corkscrew attachment on his bos'n's knife, uncorked the bottle, and took a long swash. He let out a great sigh followed by a belch and then passed me the bottle.

He seemed to have come to some sort of decision and looked me straight in the eyes. "I think we can make it, Mark. The forecast for the winds is unlike anything I've ever seen. Steady, heavy winds out of the west all the way to England. We would only need the fuel to manoeuvre the shipping lanes near Southampton, and a quarter tank is plenty. If we leave this afternoon, we could be there in less than a week."

I grinned as I lifted the bottle high in the air. An old surgical saying from residency dislodged from somewhere deep in my mind, "Persistence to the point of stupidity." Another wall had fallen and crumbled to dust in the face of persistence.

After a long guzzle of Screech, I passed the bottle back to Rufus. With my brows arched and a concerned, quizzical look on my face, I said, "That's funny, I don't taste much of anything."

There was absolutely nothing funny about that.

7 Days Earlier

November 12th, 2020

Day 6 at Sea

Voice memo #1 to Sarah:

"Sarah, we lost cell reception overnight and Rufus assures me we won't have any more until we make landfall near England. He has a satellite phone for emergencies, but there's something wrong, and it can only transmit emails, text messages, and voice memos at this point. We can't receive anything. Hopefully, he'll be able to fix it, and we can talk soon. In the meantime, this is better than nothing. I'm sorry I didn't call when we left Newfoundland and still had cell reception. I was feeling foolish because … well … you were right, I got it again – Covid. I couldn't bear to hear you say, 'Told you so.' The symptoms aren't terrible. Similar to last time with a sore throat, difficulty catching my breath, general achiness, and loss of taste and smell, but way less intense. Not sure where I got it from because I was super careful everywhere. Anyway, It's no big deal. Just a little tougher here on the boat having to stand alternating four-hour watches around the clock. Rufus seems to be okay, so far. On the plus side, we're making excellent time with speeds that Rufus has never seen before. Hope you're doing okay, and the nausea is settling down. Still can't believe we're having a baby. Okay, have to go. I'm going on watch soon. Hope you get this. Love you and I'll send another tomorrow."

I was lying on my bunk holding the sat phone and uploading my voice message to Sarah. I would only be able to send it when I was outside at the helm and the phone was in direct line of sight with the satellite. It was strange sending the message into the void with no way to know if she got it. Very much like an old-fashioned post office letter.

It was almost midnight, and I could hear Rufus fiddling with the hatch. He descended the ladder dripping water everywhere, shaking his upper body like a dog coming in from a rain shower.

"Nasty up top?" I asked, slowly pushing my virally ravaged body from my bunk, and getting ready to put my foul weather gear on. Chills ran up my bones as my stockinged feet made contact with the deck. I took a deep breath and wondered, for a moment, whether I really could survive the next four hours up top in the windy, wet, frigid night. And then I felt the thrum of the *Rumrunner* dissipate the chills and energize me.

"No, *mon*, not really." When he was tired, Rufus had a trippy Jamaican way of backing his "r" words into the word before so that "not really" sounded more like "no treally." "It's more the spray off the top of the waves from the high winds."

"The winds are still steady?"

"My friend, we are like a beautiful Mozart concerto with everything tightly interwoven to produce a masterpiece that is much greater than the sum of the individual instruments."

"So … we are on course and making good time? Is that what you're saying?"

"Yes. Incredible time. Autopilot is working well. This beautiful ship doesn't really need us, you know. We could probably both go to sleep for a week and just wake up in time to bring her alongside."

"You do love this boat, don't you?"

"Yes, *mon*, almost as much as I love my old friend Mark." He winked at me. We had grown close on this voyage, probably more so than most brothers.

He asked, "And how is Mark feeling today, with his second round of Covid?"

"I'm okay. I can't wait for my smell and taste to come back. You have some high-quality foods on board, but it's like experiencing the culinary world in washed out black and white instead of colour. That's just an inconvenience, though. Really, I'm mostly tired and rundown."

Rufus gradually removed his wet weather gear, hanging it up in the shower stall. After towelling off, he asked, "That could just be the trip taking its toll on you. No? Maybe not so much the virus."

"Probably a little of both, for sure, but I definitely have Covid. You don't forget how *that* feels. Plus, the loss of smell and taste is almost pathognomonic. Last I read, eighty percent or more of symptomatic people who test positive for Covid first experience loss of smell and taste."

"Is it normal to get it again so soon after the first time? It's only been about eight months. Right? Normally the flu only comes around once a year with a new mutated version."

"That's why they call it a *novel* virus, Rufus. It's all new to everyone, even the virologists. It could be a new mutated version, that is, a real second wave. Or it could be that the antibodies I developed after the first infection have waned and aren't effective anymore. The only way to know for sure would be to sequence the genome of the virus."

Rufus sat down at the table and removed the cork from a half empty bottle of wine that was laying sideways in netting secured to the bulkhead next to the table. It was the only way to keep bottles from rolling off the table when the *Rumrunner* started heeling. Fortunately, since we were running with the wind, this had happened rarely. He said, "Well … I don't remember everything from medical school, but I do remember that we'd need a lot more equipment than we have to run genetic sequencing."

"Hey, you'd be surprised what I can do with a propane barbecue, a shot glass, a shoelace and some Smarties."

Rufus smiled, "Yeah, MacGyver. I'm sure you could." He cleared his throat as he poured himself a "nightcap."

Now that Rufus was sitting directly under the dining table's overhead light, I was able to get a good look at him. Six days at sea took its reckoning on anyone, but he appeared … *off*. His eyes were red and swollen. His face looked puffy, and he was clearing his throat repeatedly.

"Rufus, are you okay? You don't look very good."

"*Irie, mon*, no problems. Like you, just a little tired and run down." He lifted the wine glass and swirled it repeatedly.

"You're sure? If I was exposed to the virus, then there's a good chance you may have been also."

"All good, *mon*. My Jamaican ancestral blood line is protecting me. Look," he placed his nose deep in the glass and inhaled, "notes of blackberry, cassis, and pencil shavings. See? Everything's working just –"

His eyes rolled back in his head, and he dropped like a heavy oak tree flat onto the table, his plastic wine glass ricocheting off the deck leaving a blood splatter of wine stains everywhere.

***

I remember …
"Your dad called last night, late, around 11 PM. Not long after you left for work."

"My dad? Really? All of a sudden, a decade later. Out of the blue?"

I had just woken up late-afternoon and was preparing a bacon and grilled cheese sandwich when Sarah walked through the door, home from a day's work at the hospital pharmacy. I was at the tail end of a week of nights. My circadian rhythm was upside down, and my stomach no longer knew if it was empty or full. Shift work was brutal on the body. I sat down at our kitchen island while Sarah dropped her briefcase on the floor next to Archie. He was sleeping soundly and didn't budge. She hung her coat up in the closet and then sat down opposite me.

I hesitated and then pushed my plate towards her. She grabbed half of my sandwich, and said, "I'm famished. Thanks."

"Hmm, I'm not sure that sandwich contains the right level of 'healthiness' for you."

"I don't think there's anything in the manual about that. Anyway, they already have my eggs and your … stuff."

"I suppose you're right. Are we still on for this Friday?"

"Nine AM at the clinic." We both smiled at each other and then looked at Archie, our "first born," who was lying on his back in dream state, all four paws running in slow motion, slobber dripping from his toothy grin to the floor. I turned my attention back to Sarah.

"So, what did my father say?" I leaned forward, chin cupped in hands, elbows on the island. For all my wanting to feign disinterest, I simply couldn't. I needed to know what the old bugger was up to.

"It was weird. He started off by telling me he had just retired, which we already knew from your conversation with your mother last week. And then it was like he went back in time."

"How so?"

"He was talking like it was ten years ago, in the present tense."

"Early dementia? My mum mentioned that he was showing signs?"

"Maybe. But he seemed totally lucid. It was just that he was talking like it was the day of our wedding. And although he was talking to me, it was like he was talking to you. He even slipped up a few times, calling me 'Son.'"

"What was he talking about?"

"He said his bags were packed and in his office. He hoped his tux still fit properly. It was important to look sharp. His secretary had ordered a cab to bring him to Heathrow for 10 AM. That would give him three hours to get to the hotel, changed, and be at the ceremony with time to spare."

"What did he say happened? Mum only ever told me that it was work related." *It was always work related.*

"Again, it was weird. He suddenly started yelling and swearing about, of all things, *the mumps*. 'The bloody damn mumps,' he said, over and over. And then he broke down repeating the words, 'I'm so sorry, Mark, I can't go.' Finally, he realized who he was talking to and said, 'Sarah, I'm sorry I couldn't make your wedding. It was beyond my control.' There was silence after that, and I was about to hang up when your mother came on the phone and apologized for your dad, saying he hadn't been himself lately."

"The mumps? That *is* weird." I turned to my phone.

"What are you looking up?" Sarah asked.

I read a few lines from my first hit and then replied. "Hmm, looks like on the day of our wedding, ten years ago, in 2005, England declared a national mumps epidemic."

"Think that's why your dad couldn't make it?"

"Well, mumps *is* a virus, and my dad *was* the chief virologist at Porton Down. I suppose a nationwide epidemic would involve him."

"It sounds like he was just doing his job. A very important job. Mark, you haven't talked to your father for ten years. It's time you made up." She rubbed her hands over her belly. "I don't want our future child to be estranged from his grandfather."

For a second, I considered it. But then I remembered every other missed occasion. Every other piece of my heart left in the ruins of every time I needed him. My whole body stiffened, and I lost my appetite. I pushed my half-eaten sandwich away.

"It was the mumps, Sarah. Not exactly the most complex virus and not exactly a life threatening disease, no matter how much of an epidemic it was. Surely, he had underlings who could have covered for him."

"Mark, he's reaching out. He wants to apologize to you, but you won't talk to him."

"Forgiveness after a lifetime of mistakes is something you earn. You don't just ask for it."

"You have to give him a chance. You need to reconcile your differences before it's too late."

"I don't have to do anything. Now that he's retiring and has time to talk doesn't mean I have time to listen. After all these years, he can't just waltz back into my life – our life – because he wants to."

"People change, Mark. Sometimes you have to give them a chance."

6 Days Earlier

November 13th, 2020

Day 7 at Sea

Voice memo #2 to Sarah:

"Hi Sarah. Hope you got my last memo. I don't have much time to record this one. Things have taken a turn for the worse. Rufus passed out late last night. He's got Covid, and he's got it bad. He's like a poster boy for all the symptoms. Worse than my first time, I think. He's curled up in his sleeping bag, shivering, sweating, and mumbling incoherently. He's not keeping any food or water down. I'm worried for him – *Stop. This is a bad path to be going down. There's no reason to panic her about something she can't do anything about* – but he's strong and super healthy, he'll be okay. We're still making good time and on schedule. The autopilot is working well, which is allowing me to take care of Rufus. Hope all is well. Love you."

That was a difficult message. In case something *happened* to us, I had to tell Sarah what was *happening*. She would want to know.

Things were actually much worse than the picture I had painted in the voice memo. Rufus was severely dehydrated, and I couldn't get fluids into him. I knew he had an extensive first aid kit somewhere on the ship – he was once a doctor, after all – but he never told me where it was, and I couldn't seem to find it. I was getting more frustrated by the minute. I was doing double duty on watch, and, really, I wasn't remotely qualified to handle sixty feet of ketch on my own. Fortunately, Rufus was right, the *Rumrunner* could mostly take care of herself. Which was good because I had to take care of her captain.

I had set Rufus up on a pull-out bed across from the dining table where I could keep an eye on him. I covered him with a pile of blankets that he alternatively threw to the deck and then reached for frantically when the shivering began.

I kneeled next to him and tried once more, "Rufus. Can you hear me? Where's the bloody first aid kit?"

For the first time since he passed out, he opened his blood shot, sunken eyes and looked at me. "What, *mon*?"

This was a good sign. "The first aid kit. Where do you store it?"

"Beer." Was all he said before he closed his eyes and fell into a grumbling coma/sleep again.

"Beer?" I yelled loudly, feeling thwarted once again. "That's all you can say? Beer? I wish you could keep a beer down. At least it's –"

"Wait. The locker under the forward sleeping quarters in the V berth." I ran forward and quickly ripped the Velcro fastened mattresses off the bed. Underneath were two storage compartments. I opened the hatches and peered inside. I had already looked here dismissively, not moving anything around, thinking no one in their right mind would store the first aid kit in a beer locker. Rufus was unpredictable, though, and his mind worked in strange ways at times. I lifted out case after case, until: "Eureka!" In the corner up against the hull, buried under all the beer, was a large, red emergency kit. I carefully withdrew it and placed it on the dining room table.

"Why the hell would you bury the first aid kit under the beer?" I mumbled as I opened the lid, scanned all of the contents, and quickly pulled out everything I needed to start an IV, along with two liters of saline. I rolled up Rufus' sleeve and tied an elastic strap around his upper arm. I tapped all the usual locations on his arm repeatedly, hoping for a large vein to appear. He was, unfortunately, so dehydrated that there was nothing but tiny, sinewy spaghetti veins that collapsed at the slightest pressure. Plan B: I sat him up, putting cushions under his head to allow gravity to work in my favor and then spotted my old go to – the external jugular vein. After two attempts, I successfully place a 20-gauge needle in his neck.

A Covid Odyssey Second Wave

A sigh of relief escaped my lips along with two full lungs of held breath. Intravenous access for an emergency physician – for any physician, really – can be the difference of life and death. It was the gateway to the patient's entire internal world.

I bolused a whole liter of saline in minutes and then hung a second bag off of a carved wooden handrail attached high on the bulkhead. I set the rate at a meager 75cc/hour. With all of the studies emerging about cardiac damage in Covid patients, I didn't want to overload his heart and flood his lungs.

He perked up immediately and opened his eyes. It took him a moment to focus on my face. He whispered in a dry voice, "Mark? What happened?"

"You passed out last night. Collapsed right on the table."

He attempted to lift his head off the propped-up pillows but gave up. "I passed out?"

There was a long pause as he reorganized his scrambled thoughts. "Did I spill my wine?"

I smiled, "Yeah, you made quite a mess, my friend."

He closed his eyes and put a hand to his forehead, massaging his temple. "I don't remember anything. I guess I've … I've got it?"

"You've got Covid pretty bad, Rufus."

"That's exactly how I feel – bad. Everything hurts. My throat, my muscles, my head."

"You should feel better with the all the fluids I'm giving you."

"Listen." I couldn't contain my curiosity. "Why the hell did you store the first aid kit under the beer? It took me forever to find it."

He shook his head as if he was stepping out of a net of cobwebs. "Sorry. I should have told you. I added a dozen different antibiotics to the kit for the trip. Some of them have to be kept cool. That locker with the beer in it is below water level and stays at a perfect temperature."

"Ah. And no room in the fridge. I knew your crazy mind had a reason. Any chance you've got something for Covid in there?" I asked, half joking.

"Just Camodesivir."

"Ha, ha, real funny. I guess you are feeling a little better." Rufus had the tiniest, barely perceptible, smirk on his face. Even when he was terribly ill, he still somehow retained his warped sense of humor. Camodesivir was the experimental antiviral drug that I had "borrowed" from our hospital this past March and that got me in a mess of trouble. I really didn't need to be reminded about it. Especially not right now when we were both fighting Covid.

"I am feeling a little better. How are you doing, Mark?

"Headaches still come and go, and I still get short of breath if I have to go up on deck in the wind. All in all, though, I'm recovering a lot quicker than last time."

"I'm sure I won't be so lucky."

"It will definitely take longer. You have to manufacture a whole new set of antibodies to fight the virus."

"I don't think I'll be much help on the rest of this voyage."

"Of course, you will be. You're going to tell me what to do to get the *Rumrunner* all the way to England."

"I told you, my friend, the *Rumrunner* can take of herself."

"Hmm, we'll see. How about some soup for that growly stomach of yours?"

At the mention of food, Rufus lunged for the bucket I had placed next to his bed and then dry heaved himself back to sleep. I slumped into a seat at the table, exhausted. It was hard to imagine things could get any worse.

Things would get a lot worse.

3 Days Earlier

November 16th, 2020

Day 10 at Sea

Voice memo #3 to Sarah:
Captain's log, stardate: who the hell knows ....
"Sorry, Sarah. I haven't been able to send anything for the last few days. *How many days has it been?* Rufus is coming around now, but he was in bad shape for a while. He's finally able to stand on his own two feet. I doubt you'd recognize him since he looks like he's lost twenty pounds. I'm barely holding it together myself. *Am I holding it together?* I don't think I've ever been this tired in my life, not in med school and not in residency. I'm catching cat naps wherever I

can, although not always when I want to. *Like the time I fell asleep at the wheel and the autopilot glitched putting us twenty nautical miles off course.*

"I think my Covid symptoms are mostly gone. Hard to tell with the sleep deprivation headaches and the low-grade sea sickness. The *Rumrunner* started corkscrewing a few days ago. Something to do with a slight change in the wind direction and my inability to get the rigging right. I was able to rouse Rufus long enough to help solve the problem. It messed up my inner ear, though, and left me feeling kind of green. *I was praying to the porcelain gods for almost two hours.*

"My sense of smell came back last night, just in time to stop me from eating a chicken sandwich gone bad. Turns out we blew a fuse on the fridge at some point. Had to throw out a bunch of stuff. I almost threw up when I got a full whiff of our living quarters with the body odor (can't remember the last time either of us showered), stale vomit, moldy food scraps, beer (a number of cans exploded when they were thrown to the deck during a rough patch), and toilet stench (the septic system backed up for a while before I figured out there was a secondary tank that I had to switch over to). *I was probably better off without smell. Although there is that matter of the chicken sandwich. Food poisoning would have been the kiss of death at this point.*

"On the good side, we're making amazing progress with steady winds out of the west just as Rufus predicted. Our GPS puts us at just over 500 nautical miles from the coast of the UK. Hopefully, if all continues to go well, we should be there In two days and I can see my dad – *if he's still alive* – and figure out if this cure of his is the real deal, or not. Rufus tells me this could be one of the fastest crossings under sail he's ever heard of. Guinness World Records kind of material. *Rufus did say he would get me to England in time or die trying.*

"We've had no news of the outside world since we left Newfoundland. Are there any cases at home now? Are the numbers still escalating worldwide? Or did they drop, allowing flights to open up again? I'm constantly questioning myself. Was this the right decision? Was there another way? But what's the point? There's definitely no turning back. It is what it is, and what I make of it.

"How are *you* doing, honey? Here I am, always talking about myself and what's happening on the *Rumrunner*. You're pregnant and all alone at home with Archie, holding down the fort … *Keep it together, Spencer. Keep your shit together. No tears.* I really, really miss you, Sarah. I dream of snuggling up in bed with you Sunday mornings. Just doing nothing. Just me and you, and our new baby … *No tears, dammit.* Okay, I have to go. I'm hearing a funny noise up top. Probably have to adjust the sails. Love you."

More than you could ever know.

2 Days Earlier

November 17th, 2020

Day 11 at Sea

If members of the Flat Earth Society were correct – *and they are not* – it looked as if I could swim the length of a football field over a glassy, calm Atlantic Ocean, and I would fall off the edge of the earth into … what? Oblivion? Such was the appearance of the horizon in every direction now that the winds had completely withdrawn their commitment to my mission. This was an extreme and unexpected case of *the doldrums*. That funny noise I was hearing up top yesterday evening – when I sent my last voice memo to Sarah – was the wind disappearing and the rigging slacking off. Something I hadn't heard up until that point.

"For the first time in your life, you really are in the *eye of the storm*," Rufus whispered. It was an expression I had used repeatedly throughout my life when things looked too good, and I knew disaster was lurking precariously around the corner.

The high noon sun was hanging lazily over our heads, as if it existed only for us, and it was so very quiet. After days and days of first being under motor and then under sail with near gale force winds, the absence of the usual sounds was deafening. Now, every creak and twang, every squeaky, salty hinge on the doors below deck, echoed throughout the ship.

Rufus had dismantled the radar screen and was busy piecing it back together. It's why, when the wind dropped off, we were caught by surprise. The radar had crapped out the day before, leaving us blind to anything beyond line of sight. We had motored for a while, as much to charge the batteries as to make any real headway. Now the motor was turned off to conserve fuel, and the solar panels were doing their part.

Rufus had come a long way in the last couple of days. He was upright more than horizontal and could move around the ship slowly. He was now able to drink fluids, so I removed the IV from his neck. But he still had intermittent headaches and would lose his breath scaling the ladder from below deck to the cockpit. Also, he had lost his taste and smell, along with his jovial spirit. For the first time that I could remember, Rufus was grumpy as hell. While the stagnant winds were bad for the journey, the peaceful calm was likely the best thing that could have happened for Rufus. COVID 19 and sea sickness did not mix well.

"Any luck?" I asked, hovering directly over him.

"Would be better if you weren't blocking my light," he replied curtly.

"Right." I moved to the side and peered more closely at the innards.

"Maybe it got covided," I said, raising an eyebrow, a grin on my face.

He looked at me and scowled. "It's a verb now, is it?"

"Hey, check the Urban Dictionary. It means whatever you were planning or doing got hijacked by Covid. I should know, it's happened to me enough times."

"*That* would be an appropriate word for this whole trip, wouldn't it? No fuel, no wind, radar on the fritz, getting Covid."

"I suppose. Although I'm not sure the loss of wind or the broken radar is the fault of Covid .... Your glass is definitely *moitié vide*, right now, isn't it?"

"Guess you do remember something from your time in Montreal." Rufus muttered, an edge building to his voice.

He abruptly threw a small set of pliers to the deck and stood up, wavering from side to side, as if we were still being rocked by waves. He quickly grabbed a handrail for support.

"Did you give this goddamn thing to me?" He practically spat the words at me.

"Wait? What do you mean?"

"I was very careful, always. I've travelled the world all over since March on business and never got sick. And then, I'm not with you for more than five or six days and, boom, I've got it."

"Rufus, you can't be serious."

"And you got it before I did."

"That's meaningless and depends on viral load exposure, how your own immune system is doing, and a thousand other factors. You know that."

He was really getting worked up, like I'd never seen. He held a small screwdriver in one hand, and he was tapping the butt end of it repeatedly on the top of a capstan.

"Maybe it was the old woman you met on your first plane. You said she didn't have a real mask."

"Geez, Rufus," I said, backing up slightly. "She had just come off the equivalent of a deserted island for six months. There's no way –"

"Maybe you brought it all the way from your hometown? From your emergency department, eh?"

"Our little town is the poster child of Canada for Covid cases. There wasn't one active case when I left. You know that, also."

"You said the flight attendant was very friendly. Gave you a drink. Maybe her?

"I cleaned my hands repeatedly with sanitizer on that flight. Remember, I was still freaked out from the last time I flew, coming back from Florida."

He took a deep breath. Like he had something more to say but couldn't quite put a finger on it. I took the opportunity for a rebuttal.

"Maybe you got it first? Did you think of that? From the guy who delivered our meal from Garde

Manger? Or, from one of the gas attendants where we filled up on our way up the Saint Lawrence? Hell, you could have got it long before I met up with you. The incubation period can be as long as three weeks in some rare instances."

This argument was serving no purpose other than letting off steam. We were caught in a stare down at two paces. Rufus broke off and sank heavily on to the captain's seat.

"Oh, my friend. I'm so sorry. Don't know what has come over me. I know it doesn't matter where it came from."

I sat down across from him and put my hand on his shoulder. "Look, I went through the same thing after I got back from Florida. Lying on my side in bed, rocking back and forth with every muscle in my body on fire and my guts in a wringer. You've got nothing else to do but wonder where you got it. Until you realize, it's irrelevant. An accident that's probably your own fault for not being more careful."

Rufus looked up with doleful eyes. "I was careful. Took every precaution."

"And yet, you and me both are not exactly staying locked up in our houses, protecting ourselves from the world."

Rufus reluctantly nodded his head and turned his attention back to the radar. "Where would be the fun in that?"

I clapped him on the back in agreement. "Covid is the sad price of admission these days for a life on the go."

Rufus placed the radar screen back in its proper position, secured it with four screws and fired it up.

I looked to the top of the mainmast and confirmed the antenna was spinning slow and steady.

Rufus adjusted various knobs, fine tuning it, and then paused for a moment. "Mark, do you think we will become Long Haulers?"

"Long Haulers? Where did you hear that?"

"Forbes."

"Business magazines now have articles on the long-term health effects of Covid?"

"Oh, yes. When all is said and done, Covid will have the most disastrous effects on our economy that the world has ever seen. Every business magazine has a slant on it. Ideas to make money. Lots of money."

"I should have guessed. The long-term health effects of Covid on the heart and lungs, and even the brain, will be big money-makers for some people. It seems morbid to benefit from people's misfortunes like that."

"It's reality, my friend."

An image finally appeared on the radar screen that showed us blinking on and off in the center and a fuzzy line along the western front.

What do you see?" I asked.

Rufus shook his head slowly. "Another adventure, my friend."

He looked up to the western sky, and I followed his gaze. I could see something taking shape. Something dark and ominous.

"*That* is a one-way ticket to England, Mark. Get your life vest and heavy weather gear, a storm is coming."

1 Day Earlier

November 18th, 2020

Day 12 at Sea

The *Rumrunner* was a juggernaut, piercing through some waves and arcing high off of the crests of others. The wind was at our backs once again, driving us relentlessly forward. As yet, there was no precipitation, giving us clear visibility, but we knew the heavy rains were coming. Rufus barked orders continuously as he worked the helm. It appeared the storm had knocked Covid right out of him. We had dropped two of the three foresails and reefed both the main and the mizzen. Even with less than a third of our sail square footage, we were still being pulled at breakneck speeds at times approaching 20 knots.

It was exhilarating and terrifying all at once. Schools of playful porpoises danced off the top of waves on either side of the *Rumrunner*. No matter how fast we were moving, they always seemed to have a burst of speed left in the tank to overtake us. The pace was exhausting with little time for food, drink, or sleep. Adrenaline coursed through every overworked muscle in our bodies, keeping us upright and pushing on. It felt like the slightest mistake could be the end. And then it happened.

A thunderous vibration resonated through the ship setting off a cascade of horrible events. The impact jolted up my spine and forced me into a squat, nearly propelling me over the gunnel of the cockpit like a big cannonball. If it hadn't been for my lifeline clipped onto a side rail, I would have been swimming with my porpoise friends.

Rufus had both hands locked on the helm and absorbed the shock much more gracefully. The instantaneous look of terror on his face, however, belied anything but grace. He quickly regained his captain's composure and bellowed, "Mark. Run below and check for damage. We hit something. Something big."

I unclipped, opened the hatch, and jumped down the ladder from the cockpit and into the living quarters. All the while wondering, *how could we have hit something? We're in the middle of the ocean.*

I worked my way to the bow and then slowly, on hands and knees, crawled to the stern, pausing every few moments to look, listen, and then feel, much as I would for a dying man's breath in the trauma bay.

Nothing.

I ran up the ladder and hollered over the wind, "Rufus, I can't find anything. No leaks."

Rufus shook his head. "She's not handling right. She's pulling to starboard. There must be a breach, however small."

Rufus started the engine.

"But we're low on fuel," I said.

"We're low on battery power also, my friend. If we don't keep the engine on, the generator won't charge the batteries and the bilge pumps won't work."

"You're convinced there's a hole somewhere?"

Rufus struggled with the helm to keep the *Rumrunner* on course. "I am."

If Rufus said there was something wrong with the *Rumrunner*, then I had to find it. I dropped down into the living quarters once more and this time went straight to the stern, where the engine was located. I pulled up a section of floorboard and shined a flashlight deep into the bilge. There it was: a pool of water accumulating. The smell of diesel was overpowering, and the heavy throb of the engine sent vibrations everywhere causing the pool of water to dance, like drops of water on a red-hot frying pan. The bilge pumps suddenly activated, and the water level began to drop. I moved to the area under the dining table and once again pulled up a section of floorboards. Now I could see it. A small river running from the bow to the stern on the starboard side.

There must be a breech at the starboard bow.

I pulled the mattresses off the forward V berth and removed a hatch to the compartment that contained all of Rufus' beer. Much as I had done to find the first aid kit, I moved case after case of beer until I was staring at the lower bulkhead. There was an obvious foot long gash where an intermittent spray of ocean water was pushing through. I was able to plunge my index finger through the gash, and I suddenly realized what was happening. The bow of the *Rumrunner* was rhythmically climbing over the twenty plus foot swells with the bow intermittently being above water and then below. When the bow was below water, the ocean quickly entered the breech in the hull. As long as we kept moving forward, up and down the waves, we would take on minimal water. If we came to a stop, and the bow came to its resting position with the gash below the water line, we would sink.

I tried to stuff a shirt into the gash, going for damage control, and realized it was worse than I thought. The wooden hull of the one hundred-year-old *Rumrunner* crumbled around the gash and opened even further. I had no idea what to do.

I ran back up the ladder and, huffing and puffing, explained the situation to Rufus.

"She is an old ship, Mark. The hull has been refitted many times, but the original wood is still there, weakened with time."

"What can we do?"

"We can't stop the leak, so we keep moving forward as long as we can. Keep the bilge pumps working."

"How much engine time do you think we have?"

"Six hours, give or take, but look," he pointed to the glowing orange of the radar screen, "we are on the outer edge of the storm front. Fifteen miles that way," this time he pointed forward, "we are out of the storm and in calm seas."

"If we hit calm seas with no waves to keep the bow out of the water and no engine to generate power for the bilge pumps, won't …"

Rufus couldn't look me in the eye as he said, "Calm seas are better for the Beaufort life raft."

***

We battled the elements like wild dogs around a kill. Darting and dashing, pulling in and releasing lines, up and down ladders. The rain came in hard and the waves – now twenty to thirty feet high – fattened and towered until the outside world completely disappeared when we hit the troughs, with walls of salt water so close we could almost touch them. We dropped all of the sails except the main, which remained reefed. Rufus was adamant that dropping the main completely was capitulation, defeat. If we ran out of fuel, we needed some means of forward propulsion to keep the bow out of the water.

Whenever the depth rose above a foot in the cabins, we cycled the engine on. This conserved fuel, allowing us to drain the water with the bilge pumps in one volley. It was a good strategy to buy time.

Finally, though, time ran out as the fuel tank ran dry. Only the mainsail kept us moving forward.

What little daylight there was under the grey, stormy, November skies gave way to the darkness of night. Rufus and I stood drenched in the cockpit, each with a hand on the helm, surveying the tormented scene around us as the final sputter of the engine gave way to a deep sense of hopelessness.

"Take the wheel, Mark. And do not let go. I'm going below for a moment."

"Why? There's nothing we can do about the hull breach."

Rufus gave me a sad wink I could barely make out in the red glow of our headlamps. "There's a bottle of rum I've been keeping forever in the hopes of a special occasion."

"You're giving up?" I asked.

Rufus turned to look at me as he descended the ladder. Even through the heavy rains, I could see the resignation in his eyes as a large tear rolled down his cheek. "We are in the hands of God now, my friend."

He then disappeared below deck.

Present Day

November 19th, 2020

Day 13 at Sea

Time and space coalesced into one big cauldron of unknown as I floated and bobbed under the night sky. I supposed I was lucky. The water, although just a shade above freezing, was at least calm with only the occasional train of waves trickling through, originating from some far away, unseen place. My two lifejackets were doing their job at keeping my head above water. Rarely, I would swallow the taste of a larger wave and remember to drink from my water bottles to stay hydrated. No easy feat. I'd lost all feeling below my neck and even intermittently moving my arms and legs – mostly to make sure they were still attached – did little to restore dexterity. Managing to open a water bottle in the dark, with no feeling in my hands, was an accomplishment worthy of the grandest lifesaving surgical procedure. On the plus side, I couldn't feel the pain from the lacerations to my shoulder or face, the benefits of mother nature's cryotherapy.

I dozed off and on, desperately trying to stay awake as much as possible, thinking the next time I fell asleep might be the last time – *the big sleep.* Sometimes, I sang at the top of my lungs the lyrics to every song I knew. My voice croaked out Seger, Springsteen, Dylan, nursery rhymes – anything to stay awake – until my throat parched, and I had to stop in order to conserve water. I kept a watchful eye for lights – ships, markers, anything. I had a flare gun packed in watertight plastic under my jacket. My last chance.

There was no point in swimming. *Where would I swim to?*

And then I heard it. A deep, clanging sound that was unmistakable to anyone who'd spent time on the water. The sound of a channel marker, a buoy. Ocean channel markers were far different than the relatively small ones I was used to on the Great Lakes. These were monster markers, some thirty feet high in mid-ocean. Near the English Channel, I could expect a smaller version, but still, something with a platform at the base that I could sit on, out of the water.

I swam with every dollop of self-preservation instinct I had left. Flailed was perhaps a better term, since any semblance of coordinating my muscles into actual swimming strokes was laughable. Still, I beat the water, pushed, and pulled it, dog paddled it, kicked it, spasmodically twerked it, anything that would move me towards the clanging sound. My whole world became nothing but *that* sound. And slowly, it became louder. Where there was the sound of a channel marker, there should be a green or red light. And then, I could see it, a faint blinking red light. I realized for the first time that there was mist blanketing the water which meant the buoy was closer than I could have hoped.

****

Extricating myself from the clasp of the Atlantic Ocean proved easier than I thought. With frozen limbs feeling no pain and a last spike of newly synthesized adrenaline, I hauled myself into a sitting position on the platform at the base of the marker. Aided by the intermittent red light, I MacGyvered nylon rope that I'd salvaged in the dying moments of the sinking *Rumrunner* and straps from my second lifejacket, lashing myself to the metal struts of the buoy. I then allowed my body to collapse into the restraints, hanging there, like a moth trapped in a spider web. The buoy, because of my extra weight, tilted forwards, but, like a wobbling weevil, never fell down.

Time dragged on again, counted in heartbeats, until I looked up and noticed somewhere far, far away on the watery horizon, the faintest glimmer of early dawn. I slowly turned my head from side to side and noticed that the mist had lifted. I now saw staggered lights of what I assumed to be the Southern English coastline. I reached inside my jacket and pulled the flare gun from the plastic. I aimed at forty-five degrees and then discharged it. The flare exploded and sparkled a beacon of hope. I managed to crack a painful smile from my desiccated lips and then muttered to myself as my head nodded off to the side, "Dad. I'm so close."

As the last of the adrenaline dwindled away, I slowly succumbed to a cocoon of comfortable numbness with four words looping over and over in my head, "*Damn near made it.*"

***

I went through a brief phase when I was a child where I had difficulty falling asleep because I worried I would never awaken – that I would die in my sleep.

My dad asked me, "Son. Do you dream when you're asleep?"

At the time, I had vivid, memorable dreams every night. I answered, "All the time."

He said, "If you're dreaming, you can be sure you're not dead."

Now, in my dream, I was huddled in the cuddy of a power boat with my dad at the helm and my mum at his side. We were coming home from a day trip on Windermere Lake. A frequent weekend getaway before my dad joined Porton Down. The winds had picked up, and the smell of exhaust from the old outboard was strong. I didn't mind it. Between the lull of the waves, the steady hum of the motor, and the exhaust smell, I was drifting on a comfy cloud of happy dreams.

My dad's voice echoed once again in my head, "If you're dreaming, you can be sure you're not dead."

My eyes cracked open as I caught a whiff of outboard motor exhaust. My blurry vision registered two men in a smaller Zodiac type boat tied up alongside my buoy. They were shouting at me, but I couldn't hear them. They were shaking me, but I couldn't feel them. Finally, they cut the lines holding me in place and pulled me into their boat.

This isn't a dream.

I slipped away once more and never regained consciousness until I reached the hospital.

One Day Later

November 20th, 2020

"Dr. Spencer, how are you feeling?"

"Umm. Alive?"

"Well, that's a start. Are you having much pain?" The nurse adjusted the rate of my IV as I pondered this question.

"Not enough to need meds anymore."

"Ring me if you need anything. I'll bring a lunch tray shortly." Although it was impossible to see what she looked like with her full PPE in place, including a face shield, she sounded young, and she had the pleasant, locally flavored, British accent that I remembered from this area. Something I hadn't heard in a long time.

"Sounds good. Any idea when the results of my second Covid test will be back."

"This afternoon."

I was in the "hot ward" on the medical floor of University Hospital Southampton, or UHS, as it was known. This was good, since it was only a 25-minute drive to Netley Abbey, where my parents lived. Memories of the last 24 hours were fleeting and distorted, which was probably a good thing. If you think about frozen toes in winter regaining sensation and the pain that goes along with it, you can only imagine what it feels like when your entire body goes through it. They had sedated me for long periods of time. This created a nice opportunity for the doctors to clean out, repair, and bandage the lacerations on my shoulder and face.

My IV was still running full steam in an attempt to rehydrate my weathered, scarred, frozen and thawed body. There was something ironic about floating around in a gigantic vat of ocean salt water (the origin of life and primordial soup) and suffering from dehydration. I was reminded of a poem I had studied in high school – not more than twenty miles from here – by English poet Samuel Coleridge:

"Water, water, everywhere,
And all the boards did shrink;
Water, water, everywhere,
Nor any drop to drink ..."

Fortunately, it would seem that I was going to keep all of my fingers and toes, something I recall being quite doubtful about yesterday. Apparently, during one of my more lucid moments, I had delivered the full story of my journey here, along with the fact that I'd likely had my second bout of Covid. I can only imagine the bells and whistles that went off when I had relayed this information. It was one thing to treat patients with universal precautions and another to hear from a doctor's mouth with some assurance that he has active Covid. This was a fast pass from the Emergency Department to my own personal and private isolation room here on the medical ward. Already, my Covid test from yesterday was back and was negative. Not surprising, since I'd been feeling so much better over the previous five days. I still wasn't clear if I'd been re infected from the same first wave virus, and so was able to fight it off quickly, or if I had been gifted with the new second wave mutated virus. The first scenario seemed more likely to me, given how quickly I was able to conquer it. My nurse had relayed that the doctors had been rather disappointed when I tested negative, since there had been few cases of reinfection at this point, and they were looking forward to sequencing "my virus." I did not share their disappointment.

I had been found by a deep-sea fishing trawler on its way out to work at dawn yesterday morning. They had rescued me from the buoy and brought me to the mother ship where I was wrapped in warm blankets. They then did an about face and brought me back to the Port in Southampton where an ambulance rushed me to USH. The trawler had received an all-points bulletin regarding a missing ship – the *Rumrunner* – and the Coastguard had noted an activated Emergency Position Indicating Radio Beacon – the Beaufort life raft. The Coastguard had recovered the Beaufort, but there were, apparently, no traces of the *Rumrunner ... or Rufus*.

A Covid Odyssey Second Wave

I awoke this morning famished, devouring two breakfast trays. The doctors had rounded on me, including the infectious disease specialist, and peppered me with questions about my "second wave" symptoms. There was furious head nodding and posturing, typical of the British doctors I remembered from my youth. This wasn't my first visit to USH.

Now, with my health less of a concern, I started to focus on the future. A future without Captain Rufus in it. The loss of my friend came in deep, dark waves. A complete melancholy freezing my mind until my learnt compartmentalization skills activated, and I was able to function again. I had asked the medical team this morning about Rufus to no avail. They had heard nothing. Perhaps, I hoped, if he was found alive, he had been taken to another hospital?

My nurse returned with a lunch tray, but this time she lacked the bounce in her step that I had seen earlier and moved hesitantly, unsure of herself. I fathomed a bad moon on the rise.

"Dr. Spencer." She delivered the lunch tray to my hospital table. "I have some news."

"Good? Or bad?" I asked.

"Well, both really. You asked earlier about whether or not your father was still admitted to USH?"

I hadn't spoken to my mother or Sarah in more than a week and had no idea what happened to my father. My phone was still missing along with my jacket and the rest of my clothes. Likely, a hot Covid case protocol whereby personal effects of emergency patients were stored in isolation … somewhere. The point was moot, anyway, since my phone was dead and, even if it ever worked again, would need a healthy recharge. Because I was in isolation, I wasn't allowed to use a portable landline. My nurse was kind enough to call both Sarah and my mother on my behalf. Neither picked up. That my mother didn't answer concerned me, since she never left the house. Given the time difference, I assumed Sarah was fast asleep. In both cases, a short message was delivered explaining that I'd survived the trip and was at USH.

My stomach fluttered as I asked, "Is my father here?" The crux of that question being, *Am I too late?*

"That's the good news," she responded. "He's still here in the ICU, however –"

I hated howevers.

"– he's not doing well. I spoke with the ICU attending on your behalf. Your father's been on a ventilator for almost two weeks and …"

I tuned her out as I processed mixed feelings of elation and despair: yes, after all the setbacks, I made it. I accomplished my goal. But now, I had to deal with the consequences. Two weeks on a ventilator for an elderly patient with severe COVID-19 carried an incredibly poor prognosis with a near one hundred percent chance of death.

"We are in the middle of a second surge. There's talk of taking him off the ventilator."

"Can I see him?" I asked.

"The Covid ICU is an extreme hot zone. No visitors of any kind. Plus, despite your negative test from yesterday, you're still considered to have Covid until your second test comes back.

"I'm guessing my mother wouldn't be allowed either?"

"I think you know the answer to that, Dr. Spencer."

Bells sounded from the hallway, and a muffled announcement was heard overhead.

"Bloody hell," she said, "I have to go. There's a code blue next door."

I sat for a brief time considering my options, of which there were few. I *needed* to see my father before he died. Sarah was right. I needed some kind of reconciliation, some kind of closure. I had come all this way, but the nurse was right, there was no way I would be allowed in the ICU. That left only one option.

***

I stood at the entrance of the ICU only for a moment before standing tall, like I owned the place, and pushed through the swinging doors. Memories of my efforts to rescue Sarah in the ER in Florida danced fleetingly around the periphery of my adrenaline soaked brain. During the commotion of the code blue next door, I had snagged a full PPE outfit from the entrance to my isolation room and disappeared without being seen. My hospital gown was completely hidden by the PPE. The only thing that could give me away were my paper slippers.

I had debated the ethics of undertaking this "covert operation." Having had Covid twice there was little danger to me (unless a true second wave virus lurked here, somewhere – a rare possibility and a chance I was willing to take). Having a negative test yesterday and complete resolution of my symptoms, I deemed my risk to others as virtually nonexistent particularly since I was wearing full PPE. Yes, there was a second test pending, but this was a formality. And yes, I was taking matters into my own hands, always an ethically errant thing to do. Still, I had weighed the risks versus the benefits and, right or wrong, the benefits – of me seeing my dying father and *he* potentially seeing me – won out. There are undefinable human things – thoughts and feelings – that can haunt us forever if they aren't addressed in a timely fashion.

A cacophony of noises assaulted my senses as I shuffled in. The smell of antiseptic was pervasive, and I immediately sanitized my hands. There appeared to be two sections to this particular ICU, a hot zone with ventilated patients and a hot zone where Covid positive patients were maintained on high levels of oxygen but still not intubated. Presumably, there was a whole other ICU that tended to the regular non-Covid patients. The USH clearly was in the middle of a significant surge.

I quickly passed through the non-ventilated section, where a smattering of nurses milled about performing their duties. One of the things about wearing full PPE, in particular the face shield, was that you lost sight of the world outside of your immediate focus. It was like wearing blinders, which made my stealth efforts easier. I pushed through the second set of swinging doors.

My timing was perfect. Most of the ICU nurses and at least one doctor were all gathered together at the far end of the ICU running a code on a very sick patient. The main desk was unoccupied, and I was able to glance at the patient board. I scanned it and quickly identified my father's initials, T.S. – bed 3.

A Covid Odyssey Second Wave

I grabbed a clip board for show and slowly approached my father's bed, my head bent over as if the contents of the clip board revealed vital information. I stood at the foot of bed 3 and looked for signs that my father was in it. If this was my father, there was very little left of the man I remembered. He was almost unrecognizable with, somehow at the same time, bloated and atrophied features. Weeks in bed had resulted in his muscular frame melting away. His limbs and face were edematous and elephant-like from retained water. A tube – like a proboscis – protruded from his mouth and snaked to a sophisticated ventilation machine that controlled his breathing. The steady whirring of mechanical gears pumped air, keeping him alive.

Is this really my father?

I closed my eyes in disbelief and then looked closely at a monitor where his full name was displayed: Thomas Mark Spencer.

I donned gloves and approached the bed side. His arms were severely bruised from multiple IV and blood drawing efforts, and his skin was paper thin, likely from the steroids he was receiving. I put my hand on his and held it, wondering if he could hear anything. A heaviness formed in my chest and my limbs turned cold. One of my many walls fell as I metamorphosed from doctor to son, and the tears fell with it, hidden behind my mask and shield.

"Dad, it's Mark." I whispered just loud enough to be heard above the sounds of the ventilator. "I got your letter, and I came to see you. It wasn't easy, but I made it. I haven't seen Mum yet and I haven't been to your basement ..."

His eyes flickered and he moved a finger. He clearly wasn't paralysed, and if they were thinking of taking him off the ventilator, they were likely weaning him off of the sedatives. Maybe?

"Dad, can you hear me? It's Mark."

He turned his head just a little from side to side and scrunched his cheeks.

The commotion had died down where the code was being carried out. Nurses were heading back to their respective patients. I didn't have much time.

It was stupid how hard it was to say it, even right here and right now. The old habits were like concrete, weighing everything down, and I had to lift hard to get it out.

"Dad, I don't have much time and I need to tell you something. I miss you and … I love you."

Footsteps approached slowly from every direction.

My dad's eyes suddenly opened just enough that I could see his pinpoint pupils and a stream of tears pour out. We connected for a brief moment before his heartbeat sped up uncontrollably and went into V-tach. This was quickly followed by a flat line on the monitor. There were no buzzers, no bells; he had a "do-not-resuscitate bracelet" on his wrist. There was nothing I could do but hold his hand as he collected his angel wings and Crossed the Veil.

I whispered in a choked voice, "Goodbye, Dad." And then I backed away as nurses began to take notice on monitors at the main desk that something was amiss at Bed 3.

***

I slid through the swinging doors undetected into the adjacent, less critical ICU section where the hissing of flowing oxygen permeated the room. I shuffled trance-like passed bed after bed of Covid patients, all of whom could suffer my father's fate at any moment. I wanted to bolt. To get the hell away from this hospital. I was on the balls of my feet, ready to run, when I heard it.

An unmistakeable, deep, gregarious, muffled laugh.

I stopped in my slippered tracks and looked towards its source. The oxygen mask and bandages around the man's face could not disguise the red Rastafarian dreadlocks protruding from beneath a hair bonnet.

"Rufus!"

Two Days Later

November 21st, 2020

I stood weary and fatigued in front of my old house on number 9 Chamberlayne Road, carrying my backpack at my side. I stared for what seemed like an eternity at the front door.

Finding Rufus alive had been a temporary antidote to the despair I was wallowing in after watching my father die. I didn't have time to get the full story, but Rufus had been found washed ashore and brought to USH. He was unconscious until early this morning, and, without his wallet – which was still sitting in the outside pocket of my weather jacket – they had no way of identifying him. The damage that the freezing water had done to his body was extensive, hence all the bandages that were covering frostbitten wounds. He was told that he would probably lose a few toes, a fair payment for surviving such an ordeal.

His bigger problem, though, was Covid. He was having a tough time fighting it off and was requiring significant oxygen. This, too, however, was improving, and I had no doubt he would make a full recovery. I had been able to sneak back into my room with no one the wiser and, at my insistence, once my second Covid test came back negative, was given all of my belongings and discharged.

I still hadn't heard from Sarah, but I had managed to contact my mother. She knew I was coming.

Seeing the carefully crafted, oversized solid oak entrance with its large lion head door knocker – an exact replica of the Prime Minister's at 10 Downing Street – brought back a flood of memories. This was the same door I'd opened and closed a thousand times – a million times? – on my way to and from school; to and from activities of all sorts; to and from life outside the family world. While I was certain there were some bad memories, all I could think of were the good ones. The sound of a clutch engaging, and the smell of exhaust snapped me out of the moment as my cab departed. I hadn't seen my mother in many years, and, on the one hand, I was longing to reach the end of my journey – the second brown envelope in the basement, on the other, my father had just passed, and she would surely be devastated and in need of comforting.

I climbed the five steps and hesitated with my hand over the knocker, my mother frequently left the door unlocked during daylight hours. I tried the handle, pushed, and the door gave way to the scents of my childhood. If seeing the door had stirred memories, the smells of leather and books, oil paints, and daffodils opened a floodgate to my past life in Britain. There was another smell though, a new one I'd never noticed before. An odor that accompanied nursing home patients that I saw in the ER: the smell of aging. I crossed the threshold and shouted, "Mum?"

I heard a rustling sound in the kitchen, footsteps, and then my mother appeared. She was dressed immaculately and fully made up, as if she were meeting royalty for lunch. She was fairly stooped over, much more so than I remembered, and considerably shorter as a result. She approached me and stopped short, six feet away. Her shoulders were hiked and standoffish, like I was a stranger.

"Mark! Close the door. It's cold outside. Don't want to catch pneumonia, or … something else."

I could see she was hesitant, not quite sure what to do with me. "Mum, it's okay, I was tested at the hospital. Twice. I'm negative now."

"You were at USH. You were sick with Covid on that dreadful sailboat, weren't you?" Her voice was fearful and accusatory.

"I was. But remember, that was my second time. I recovered much quicker. I'm safe to be around."

Her husband of 54 years had just succumbed to the disease. She was angry and I could see her survival instincts were primed.

"You're sure?"

"They wouldn't have let me leave the hospital to come see you if I were sick and contagious."

That was what she needed to hear. Her face softened and her shoulders relaxed. She smiled and teared up simultaneously and then stepped towards me faster than I thought possible for a seventy-four-year-old woman. She embraced me in a warm hug and whispered, "So good to have you home, Mark. We missed you."

***

My mother prepared lunch, and we sat for half an hour catching up, making plans for my father's burial – or, in any case, what plans you could make in these times of social distancing and restricted gatherings. She made me remove the bandage from my cheek and told me that the laceration made me look more rugged and handsome. I wasn't sure Sarah would agree.

I recounted parts of my journey to come home. She smiled as she said, "You always did attract trouble when you were a boy."

"One boy's trouble is another boy's adventure," I countered.

"You haven't changed at all, have you?"

"I *am* going to be a father now. Maybe that will change me."

"Mmm, I doubt it."

She continued, "Speaking of fathers, I think it's time we visited the basement."

Strangely, after everything I'd gone through to get here, I really didn't want to move from this place of safety, here in *my* old kitchen, sitting in *my* old chair, across the table from *my* mother. I was suddenly a child again, protected from the dangerous world outside.

I finished the last of my tea, released a long sigh, and then pushed my chair back from the table. It was time to be an adult again.

My mother escorted me to the basement entrance, produced a very old key that unlocked the door and then stood to the side.

"You're not coming down?"

"Your father wanted you, and you alone."

"But surely you're curious?"

"I am, but I'll give you some time before I come down."

I gave her another hug, turned an ancient doorknob, and pushed the door open to the sound of creaky hinges desperately in need of oil. Musty, damp, basement smells drifted upwards as I reached in to turn on the light switch. I retraced the footsteps of my father down the old stairs trying to suppress conflicting emotions and thoughts. Did my father, a former world class virologist, really discover the cure for COVID-19? Or was this all the elaborate trappings of a demented mind in progressive cognitive decline. I slowly continued my descent.

Based upon my mother's description of the many men and old colleagues carrying box after box to the basement at the beginning of the pandemic, and the many references my dad had made to "his lab," I fully expected a functioning experimental workspace and laboratory, the kind I had seen a few times when I visited him at the university before he joined Porton Down. This was not the case. Not at all. I had never asked my mother what she saw when she came down to look for the envelope the first time we spoke, and I had let my imagination run wild.

As I rounded a corner on the stairs, the full area of the basement came into view and I froze, completely astonished. There were no containment areas or biohazard suits. No gleaming metallic work surfaces covered with microscopes, test tubes, and chemistry type equipment. No laboratory equipment of any kind. There was only a very long, wide table – the kind you might find at a castle banquet in days gone by – with absolutely nothing on it. As I scanned the room which, as with the rest of the house, was entirely done up in Victorian era varnished oak, giving it that dark library look, I saw stack after stack of either books and journals, or boxes – presumably filled with books and journals – lining the walls and scattered everywhere across the floor. A dolly sat in one corner. Only the table was cleared of all things word related.

My heart sank. I had really wanted my father to be that superhero-like guy who, against all odds, discovered the cure for the deadly virus in the basement of his home, while the rest of the world came up empty, working in the best labs. *He had dementia, for God's sake. Some days he could barely tie his shoes.*

As I stepped off onto the concrete floor, I noticed, embedded into the larger bookcase on the far wall, the one thing that looked completely out of place amongst all of these writings: a large black safe. It was recessed into a bookcase with the shelves built out all around it. I approached it somewhat hesitantly, curiously. *Would the envelope be there? Was all of this a fool's errand?*

I walked towards it, weaving my way amongst the boxes on the floor, until I stood directly in front. My eyes suddenly widened, and my brow furrowed.

On the shelf directly above the safe I could see – not books or journals – but plastic and wooden models of all sizes and shapes. *My models. The ships, planes, and everything else of my childhood.* I ran a gentle finger over the fuselage of the first Spitfire I'd ever built and along the dusty sails of the H.M.S *Victory*. There was even my Apollo 11 Lunar Module, with the gold tinfoil wrapped around its base. *The old bugger. He kept all of them.*

I took a deep breath and then focused my attention on the safe. It stood half my height and about three feet wide. The door, as my mother suggested, had some sort of biometric scanner that was bathed in the pale glow of a steady, small red light. I wasted no time in putting my thumb on it. A whirling of gears disrupted the dark silence as latches gave way and the light turned green. Next to the scanner on the door was a spoked wheel that reminded me of a miniature version of the helm on the *Rumrunner*. I placed both of my hands on it, turned counterclockwise and pulled. The hefty door opened with a woosh of air as the vacuum seal broke. I crouched down and peered inside. On the top shelf lay a large book. It was the only thing in the safe. I lifted it out and carried it over to the long, empty table, winding my way through a small path bordered on either side by stacks of books and boxes, and then sat down in my father's chair. I felt the leather give as I sank into it and my hands brush up against the worn edge of the table that I vaguely remembered sitting and playing on as a child, during those rare occasions that I had been allowed into the basement. I softly set the book on the table, afraid to disturb the silence of a lifetime's worth of intellectual pursuit. I couldn't escape the feeling that my dad was watching me.

I ran my fingers over the blank cover and realized it wasn't really a regular book at all but a scrap book collection of photographs. One I had never seen before. Sticking out at the top, was the edge of an envelope, placed like a book marker. I opened the book to the marked page and beheld a brown envelope very much like the one that was mailed to me – what seemed like a lifetime ago. On it, my name was scribbled.

I undid the red filament tie, opened the envelope, and removed a thickish document entitled, "SARS-CoV-2 gene therapy model by Dr. Thomas Mark Spencer." I leafed through it and could see where the page that he'd sent me had come from. It was all very complex and detailed, and I read through it carefully.

Certainly not the ravings of a demented imagination.

In essence, he seemed to have discovered a way to combine DNA-encoded antibodies with the science of gene therapy. He had worked out a way to harvest a sample of antibodies from a patient infected with SARS-CoV-2, reverse engineer the genetic code that produced those antibodies, meld that genetic code into a non-Covid type, deactivated virus (much like those used in cancer gene therapy) and then inject the new, genetically modified virus into the muscle of a sick patient, where that virus' modified DNA would combine with the patient's native muscle cell DNA and, in a factory like way, quickly produce the new anti-

Covid antibodies necessary to fight off the illness. I placed the document back on the scrapbook and pondered. It was pure genius. And if it worked, the technology could not only be used to fight SARS-CoV-2, but any virus!

I looked around the room at the incredible number of books and journals, realizing that he'd likely read every one of them many times over and, suddenly, I had an epiphany. This was a "thought" lab. When my father referred to his "lab," he wasn't referring to an "experimental" lab, he was referring to his "thought" lab. A lab where he carried out thought experiments. He always said that the heavy lifting of science was never in the *doing* but in the *thinking*.

I stood from the table and this time did a full 360-degree sweep, taking it all in. I reached over to one of the stacks and pulled an article off the top and looked at it. It happened to be one that my father had authored and published decades ago in the New England Journal of Medicine on the theoretical concepts of using viral vectors in gene therapy. His theory had now become reality in cancer treatment.

Was this why you needed me to come here, Dad? You could have easily mailed that second envelope, but you needed me to see all of this, your thought lab? All the mental work that went into producing this document. *So that I could believe you when no one else would.*

I picked up the document once again off of the scrapbook, and suddenly, it weighed a million pounds. If he'd really done it, his ideas would save millions of lives.

"That one was his favorite," my mother said.

"You snuck up on me. I didn't hear you come down." It was like she had materialized at my side.

"You were deep in thought."

"I suppose I was."

She placed her arm around my waist. "Your father used to say that when he was deep in thought, it was like he was travelling to the future since it was suddenly hours, or sometimes days later, when he would rejoin our world."

"Yes, I remember him always saying, 'Is it already tomorrow?'"

"Your father had a good life, although it probably passed faster than he would have liked."

"The downside of being a time traveller, I guess."

We both smiled, and the tension in the room suddenly eased.

"You said, '*that one* was his favorite.' What one?"

"That picture under the envelope."

I hadn't even noticed it. I looked down and moved the envelope and document completely to the side. Under it was a large picture of me straddling my father's shoulder in a meadow standing in front of the Stonehenge monument. He had a joyous smile on his face.

"That was when he was most happy, before he joined Porton Down."

My mother continued, "He may not have said it much, or ever, Mark, but your father truly loved you."

I pulled the picture from the scrapbook and stared at it, a tear escaping from the corner of my eye. I turned it over and, scrawled on the back in my dad's handwriting, it said, *"So proud of you, Mark. Love you."*

Suddenly, I wondered if the real purpose of my journey wasn't simply to see this picture and read those words.

Five days later

November 24th, 2020

"I can't believe you actually own a *Jet Aiiiiiiirliiiiiiner,*" I sang. I was still riding a high from the discoveries in my dad's basement lab. And I was excited to get home. And I was on a private jet for the first time in my life.

"Well, Steve Miller, there are some perks to being filthy rich," Rufus answered.

"Why the hell didn't we just take your plane to England in the first place?"

"The borders weren't just closed to commercial flights. It was all flights, including private."

"You're telling me with all your money, influence, and connections, you couldn't work your way through the red tape?"

"Possibly, but it might have taken several days, or even weeks, and I couldn't be sure. Plus, I needed to get the *Rumrunner* across, and it was good to have a friend on board to share the adventure with, for a change."

I gave Rufus a skeptical look. We were buckled in to two very plush, comfortable swivel seats taxiing to the runway on Rufus' private Gulfstream. Rufus' hands and feet were still bandaged. He still had all his toes (for now) and was stable enough to travel and get definitive medical management closer to home. Dealing with frostbite type injuries was often a waiting game. His second Covid test had come back negative this morning and his Gulfstream was standing by.

We had talked briefly by phone, but I hadn't seen him since I'd left the hospital, and he had just arrived by wheelchair, so we really hadn't had a chance to catch up since the sinking of the *Rumrunner*. I could tell he was still grieving. Losing the *Rumrunner* was like losing a family member for him. When Rufus was unhappy, he lost his jubilant Jamaican accent and reverted to, what I called, his medicalese speech, the kind he had used in medical school when he was giving a talk with staff in the audience, like Grand Rounds.

"Rufus, I'm really sorry about the *Rumrunner*. She was a fine, fine ship with amazing character. It was incredible that she lasted as long as she did in that fluke storm."

"Just long enough to get us close enough to the shipping channels and give us a chance. Very fortunate. I will miss her greatly."

"I almost forgot," I said. "I have something for you." I reached into my backpack and removed a small plastic bag which I passed to Rufus. "I'm afraid it's still a little damp."

Rufus opened the bag with fumbling, bandaged fingers and looked inside. "My wallet! You grabbed it from the cubby hole before the *Rumrunner* sank." He pulled a favorite photo of the *Rumrunner* from it and then looked at me with one bushy eyebrow raised. "Why did you bother?"

I grinned, "I knew we'd be seeing each other again."

Rufus released a long, heavy sigh. "My friend, I'm glad one of us had faith."

A flight attendant approached and straightened our chairs for take-off. The Gulfstream accelerated and, smoother than any plane I had ever been on, took to the skies. Once we were at cruising altitude, I turned my chair back to face Rufus. We had a lot to discuss. He leaned in towards me, grimacing as he held his hands in the air like a surgeon or nurse after scrubbing. "So," he asked, "you found your holy grail. The cure."

I smiled. "Possibly. It looks promising. I've sent a scan of the document my dad left me to some colleagues to look over."

In fact, at first, I really wasn't sure what to do with the document. It was hard to imagine any government agency would take me seriously, let alone a major pharm company. Eventually, I decided I needed to verify the authenticity of my dad's research before I did anything else. Given what The Hitchhiker had said when last we spoke, just before the *Rumrunner* sank, he seemed as good a place as anywhere to start. I had emailed the scanned document to him and was still waiting for a reply. Covid numbers throughout the world were on a steep rise again, and I was hopeful for a quick response.

"Maybe, you and I, we go into the pharmaceutical business together, *mon*. You can buy your own Gulfstream."

There was that "*mon*" I was looking for. Rufus was on the mend. There was nothing like a business opportunity to get him back on track.

"You'll be the first person I contact, if it turns out to be something real, Rufus. Trust me."

Rufus had obliquely made an interesting point. One I hadn't given much consideration to, yet. If my dad's work really led to a cure, not just for Covid, but potentially all viral infectious diseases, it would be worth a fortune. I suddenly felt nervous about the document I was carrying in my backpack, casually tossed onto another seat. Not to mention, since I'd sent it to The Hitchhiker, it was now already floating around in the cloud. Although I trusted him implicitly, *people* could hack email accounts. My paranoia was starting to spiral when Rufus' phone rang. He said very little, listening intently, and then gently tapped out, ending the call. He looked up at me, his eyes moist and confused, his joyous self once again subdued.

"I think I know where we got the Covid from."
"You do?"

A Covid Odyssey Second Wave

"That was one of my other partners in that new facemask company I was investing in. Charlie Treemont died yesterday."

***

Rufus and his Gulfstream dropped me off at the Toronto Pearson Airport, as if we'd just come back from a night out at a hockey game, and he was giving me a lift home in his car. Because of Covid restrictions and coming from overseas, his pilot wasn't able to obtain permission to bring me all the way home.

We should have slept on this red eye flight, but it was impossible after hearing about Charlie Treemont. We spent the night talking, trying to make sense of it. Charlie had told me on the flight to Montreal that he'd been recently tested. He must have caught it sometime after that and before he met Rufus and I (if it was indeed Charlie who passed it on to us – *who could really know for sure?*). He had already caught the first wave infection in April and would have had some degree of immunity. That made it highly probable that he was killed by a true second wave infection: a new, more deadly, more contagious, mutated coronavirus. I remembered being overtaken by a head to toe chill when we came to this conclusion. Rufus shook his head repeatedly and said, "Oh, my friend. And there we were in the bar, carrying on, *maskless* .... This is all very bad. Very bad."

I wished with all my heart that Charlie could take back his words, *"I'd just as soon get the second wave now and get it over with."*

When the morning came, we watched the sunrise as we landed in Toronto and then said our goodbyes. Rufus was heading back to Montreal where he would get further medical care.

I was sitting in a twin prop plane with all the comforts of the Gulfstream left in the clouds behind. There were very few people onboard this time. Like the disease itself, word of the second wave was spreading rapidly. Waiting at the gate, I had scrolled the local news. Lockdowns were being reinstituted everywhere: schools were closing, hospitals were in crisis, restaurants were open for take-out only and retail stores by appointment only. In fact, with no end in sight, many restaurants and stores were closing down forever. It was the whole shebang from March all over again except that the vise was being screwed tighter, a lot tighter.

As always, I had wiped down my seat and the area within arm's reach. Coincidently, this was the same plane and seat that I started my journey on. As we were taxiing away from the gate, before I turned my phone off, an email came through. I thought it was Sarah, but it was something completely unexpected. It was from someone named May Fitzpatrick:

Dear Dr. Spencer,

You don't know me, but I'm June Fitzpatrick's sister. I was going through her email contacts and came across yours. Although I don't remember if you were one of the many physicians involved in her medical care over the past two weeks at Henry Ford, in case you were, I wanted to thank you. She didn't suffer, and that's what mattered most to me. Covid is a terrible disease with terrible complications, but all of you were there for her from start to finish. You are the best of our society devoting your lives to saving our sickest people.

Thank you.

Sincerely,

May Fitzpatrick

I looked over at the seat where June and I sat not three weeks ago connecting over thoughtful discussion. She was a beautiful person. I turned my head to look out the window, slouched deep into my chair and pulled my baseball cap down tightly over my eyes. I felt like I was standing naked on a beach staring up at the biggest wave I'd ever seen. It stood there, in place. The waters writhing freely within the wave but not advancing. And then something released, and it came crashing down. My world breaking into a million painful pieces, each little piece fitting together to make up the last three weeks of my life.

The tears were cathartic, and I sobbed quietly with my head against the window for the remainder of the flight home. If only June could have stayed on her little island.

Home

November 24th, 2020

I drove my Highlander through a thin dusting of fresh snow as bright sunshine quickly turned the new snow into puddles. I glanced at my well-worn mask dangling by one ear strap from my rear-view mirror and breathed a sigh of relief: I was almost home. As per our phone conversation when I was in Toronto, Sarah had left my SUV at the airport an hour earlier with the keys over the passenger rear tire. There would be no quarter given for any possibility of infecting Sarah or our unborn child.

My emotions were a kaleidoscopic acid trip of fun house mirrors on the drive home: disorganized – *are emotions ever organized?* – and out of control – *do we control our emotions, or do they control us?* Hearing of June's passing had put a kink in my happy return and distant melancholy was the last thing Sarah needed. I had to be fully present to experience her wrath all in one shot, or it would drag out forever – tiny cuts metered out to every part of my psyche. She had vehemently opposed my boarding Rufus' sailboat, and now I had to atone for that unilateral decision. Did the end justify the means? In the long term, probably – *maybe?* – if a cure came from it. In the short term, though, I had to pay the price for my tunnel vision. I fully expected Sarah to be equal parts pissed and equal parts elated at my return, particularly since my mission was mostly successful – *for Christ's sake, I may have the cure for Covid and any other viral infectious disease in my little black backpack* – and, well, I didn't die in the process.

While I was still in England, Sarah and I had caught up with extended, daily FaceTime calls. These were some of the most difficult conversations we'd ever had. For whatever reason, she had never received my voice memos – presumably they were still bouncing around the stratosphere on a journey to nowhere. After ten days with absolutely no communication, she had assumed the worst, and who could blame her? I certainly couldn't. The day before we were rescued, she had called the police, who called the Canadian Coast Guard, who liaised with Her Majesty's Coastguard …. Sarah had stayed awake all night with her phone in hand, waiting. I felt horrible for her.

Still, after being on the receiving end of her hellfire rage for more than an hour, I had to defend myself a little bit – *The cure. Hello?* – and this made matters even worse. Apparently, although my pigheaded brain could not appreciate it, I was worth more to her than *the cure*. It wasn't until the end of our second call that the strain began to dissipate, and our conversation approached some level of normalcy. Strangely, it was talking through my dad's passing that created some neutral ground. For all his eccentricities and workaholic attitude, she loved my dad and felt every bit the loss that I did. Everything else, however, still remained on shaky ground.

June and Charlie's passing? She didn't know them, but I did, and the pain of their deaths was still very fresh. I sat at a red light and stared into the rear-view mirror for a moment practicing my happy place smile. *Fake it 'til you make it.*

Arriving at my house and parking in the driveway proved shockingly comforting, like I'd just passed over a draw bridge and into safety behind castle walls. I lumbered up the stairs, exhausted from my travels, reminded of coming home from my first day back at work three weeks earlier. My backpack hung from a slack arm at foot level, thumping on each step. I stood at the front door and paused, sucking in a long breath of fresh northern air. It would be my last for fourteen days. Even if I was tested again and was negative, Sarah was adamant that I would be in quarantine for the duration. Again, no quarter given.

The door was open, and I stepped into the alcove. I dropped my pack to the floor and stripped off all of my clothes, including my underwear and socks. I suspected she would burn everything. I put on the waiting housecoat and slippers, tucked my cell phone into my housecoat pocket and pulled the document from my backpack, gripping it tightly in my hand. Through the draped window of the alcove door, I could see the blurry outline of my wife down the hall. I opened the door and gingerly stepped through.

She stood with her arms crossed – Sarah style, with both hands buried in her armpits – her beautiful hair was tied back, and she had her glasses on, a sure sign that she'd been crying. My gut ached with want – to run to her, to hold her. But I knew better, as did she. Our logical minds were in complete control. I could hear Archie yelping behind the kitchen door, pulling at my heartstrings. Another slice in the chainmail under my armour.

"Honey, I'm home," said I, my voice trailing off.

"You get your ass upstairs, you big …"

There was a long breathless moment where I could hear every sound in our ancient house: Archie whimpering, the furnace pushing air, the creak from my weight on the floor as I shifted from side to side, the wind blowing off the river into the bay windows, the thump of my heart beating against my rib cage.

I looked up from where my gaze had fallen to the floor. "I'm sorry. I'm sorry about what I put you through, Sarah."

"I'm sorry, too, Mark. About your father and … everything."

We both stood at a distance with our watery eyes locked and our cheeks drenched with loving tears.

"Now get your god damn, tired, sorry ass upstairs to the attic where it belongs."

I bounded for the stairs and began the long climb to my prison tower. I felt just that little bit lighter, able to take two and three steps at a time.

She yelled up. "You look like shit by the way."

"You look amazing," I yelled back.

"I'm going to burn all your clothes."

"I knew you would."

"And don't touch anything on your way up."

"I wouldn't dream of it …"

The door to the attic was left open, so I wouldn't touch the doorknob, and I climbed the last set of stairs.

I surveyed my cellblock. Sarah had set it up beautifully. My memory foam pillow was on the bed and there were even flowers. A small refrigerator had been moved from the basement, full of refreshments. All in all, it seemed doable. Maybe even enjoyable.

She had placed my laptop on the desk. I flipped it open, and while it downloaded several hundred emails, I pulled a celebratory ale from the small fridge, raised it to the ceiling in a pantomimed toast and downed a well-earned swig.

***

Later that afternoon, I stood deep in thought staring out a window that overlooked St. Mary's River, still in my housecoat. The sun was gleaming off thin patches of ice that had formed on the river. My thoughts turned to the kayak adventure that had set everything off. What was for me the start of Covid, ground zero.

Earlier, Sarah had brought up my perfect comfort lunch: mac'n cheese with bacon and a glass of chocolate milk. She had sat on the lower flight of stairs, and we talked for an hour before she told me she needed a nap and strongly suggested I do the same since I looked exhausted. She further highly recommended I have a shower saying she could smell the travel stink from below. It sounded like I'd been forgiven, but that I would be a guinea pig for mother-nagging until the baby was born.

A small price to pay for deeds questionably performed.

My introspective moment was abruptly intruded upon by a ringing sound from my laptop. I moved to my desk and looked at the screen. Someone was facetiming me. I sunk into my swivel chair and moused the accept button. The screen filled with a face I absolutely didn't recognize, until he spoke.

"I see you survived the sinking boat."

"Hitchhiker?"

"Your father's research checks out. I've reviewed it extensively with experts in the field that *I* respect."

Since making his acquaintance earlier this year, I had discovered that there were very few people in the world that were privileged of The Hitchhiker's fulltime-intellectual respect.

"That's, that's incredible." It sounded too good to be true. There had to be a catch: An "except for." Or an "as long as." Or another "shoe to drop."

"You look horrendous. Like you haven't slept in weeks."

"Well, I haven't. It's been quite an –"

"And why are you wearing a housecoat in the middle of the afternoon? There's work to be done."

"I'm in quarantine. I'm up in the –"

"In quarantine? Why? You've already had the first wave coronavirus."

"Actually, I may have got the second wave version of the virus also, while on the sail –"

"All the more reason why you shouldn't be in quarantine. Aren't you a doctor? You should know this."

"Well, I did test negative twice before leaving – "

"Exactly. Stop this nonsense. There's work to do."

"But Sarah is pregnant and she insis –"

"That's completely illogical and ridiculous. As I said, there's work to do. The lives of many are at stake."

"Hmm. I guess I can discuss it with –"

"There's a problem. Something's missing."

"Wait. What?" I could hear the sound of that other shoe dropping.

"Your father's research was impeccable, truly a brilliant man. It's all there in the document. Save for one thing he couldn't have anticipated. For lack of a better word at the moment, there's an 'ingredient' needed to incorporate the gene modified viral vector into the patient's muscle. That 'ingredient,' although somewhat rare, is typically imported in abundance here in the US. It's used to carry out certain gene therapy experiments. As it turns out, with Covid in full force, a plethora of studies are being carried out across the states requiring this same 'ingredient.' As a result, there is a dramatic shortage. In fact, according to my sources, there's none left. Anywhere."

"Anywhere?"

"Nowhere. Except for where it's sourced."

Deep down, I really didn't want to know.

"Fifty miles north of Wuhan near a small town called Xiantao is a factory that produces the entire world's supply of this 'ingredient' from a rare plant that exists only in that one place."

"Wuhan?"

"It's not ironic, if that's what you're thinking. It's just coincidence that the ingredient required for the potential cure can only be found immediately next door to the suspected origin of the virus."

It sounded terribly ironic to me. A deadly irony that was looking down upon me with vitriolic eyes from somewhere high above the earth. The shoe that dropped seemed to have landed directly on top of me.

I was staring at the screen, speechless. What words could possibly convey my dismay. My sheer and utter, world-crushing disappointment.

"Why did you shave off your beard and mustache?" I asked, stalling for something worthier to say. In a rare moment of regular, linear conversation, The Hitchhiker answered my question.

"It was necessary to allow a proper mask fit. This pandemic is here to stay for a good while."

"Oh. Makes sense." It was why I hadn't recognized him when he first appeared on the screen. I'd never seen him without a beard. A bus suddenly whizzed by behind him and I could hear the squeal of heavy brakes. For the first time, I realized he was outdoors, and I could see his breath."

"That's my ride," he said.

"Wait. Where the hell are you?"

"Outside of a coffee shop pirating Wi-Fi for this FaceTime call."

"You're taking the bus? You never take the bus. You always hitchhike."

"I'm tracking down a lead that could help. Time is precious. I'll contact you as soon as I have something."

The Hitchhiker disappeared before I could say another word, and I was left staring deep into the emptiness of a black screen, a blank slate where the third part of my journey was already taking shape. June, Charlie, and my dad were all dead from this terrible COVID-19 virus. I had to see it through to the end.

Sarah yelled from below, "Honey, are you up? Dinner's ready and on the landing. I just got off the phone with my sister. Can you believe she's still seeing that philandering orthopod, Rick?"

But, for now, a little normalcy was exactly what the doctor needed.

The End

Author's Notes

As mentioned in the subtitle, this is a work of fiction. That being said, most of the information, medical or otherwise, is real. The following are clarifications on certain topics of interest:

The medical views presented in this novel are current as of November 2020. One of the caveats of writing a medical novel based on true events *during* those events, is that it gives the reader a snapshot in time of the beliefs of the medical community at the time of the writing. Further, information changes rapidly, and what was factually true when this book was written may not be true even six months from now. The evolution of the use of gloves is a perfect example. When the first book in this series was written in June 2020, the use of gloves was considered essential to prevent transmission by reducing the spread of fomites. Six months later, when Second Wave was written, research had determined that washing your hands was superior to wearing gloves. Medical information is a continuously evolving science.

Masks, masks, masks. This is certainly one of the most controversial aspects of Covid and continues to evolve at warp speed. The facts presented in this book represent my understanding of the literature and leading experts as of the end of November 2020. Most certainly, ideas on proper mask utilization have changed since then. I would advise the WHO website for up-to-date information on this topic.

The "cure" that I have proposed in the document, "SARS-CoV-2 gene therapy model by Dr. Thomas Mark Spencer" is largely fictitious but based on current research as discussed in an article published June 18th, 2020, in the MIT Technology Review by Antonio Regalado titled: *Here's how genes from covid-19 survivors could help you – Gene therapy could put an end to future pandemics*. It is available online and definitely worth reading.

I took some liberties with the timing. Effective 1st October 2020, Transport Canada banned all masks with valves or vents from all Canadian airports and planes. As well, bandanas, neck gaiters and face shields were banned at that time.

I noted an infection rate of 28/246 passengers on the flight Mark took from Florida in March 2020. This would be considered exceptionally high by today's standards and reflects a time before appropriate protection was in place on a flight coming from a hot zone. At present, only passengers within two rows of an infected individual would be considered high risk and, even then, very few would test positive.

Counterintuitively, flying is surprisingly safe at this time.

Regarding vaccines and the topic of vaccine hesitancy, a more recent Pew Research Center poll conducted between the 18th and 29th November 2020, showed that 60% of people 'probably' or 'would' take the vaccine if it were available at that time. These numbers are obviously subject to significant variability, depending on the timing of the study relative to confidence in research and development processes of the COVID-19 vaccines.

It was difficult to know where to end this Author's Note since there is so much more I could discuss. However, I must leave something to write about for the next book ☺

Acknowledgements

A special thanks to my wife, Andrea, for her ongoing and eternal encouragement, as well as to my children, Emily and Charles, for their insightful feedback.

My writing partner and longtime friend, Laura Cody – I wouldn't have made it this far without her help.

Cynthia Clement for her detailed experience with the publishing process (check out her many books on Amazon!).

Vicky Willet for access to her incredible knowledge base of COVID-19 information.

Dr. Brynlea Barbeau for her compassionate words of wisdom on the subject of substance use disorders.

Capt (N) (Ret'd) Kim Kubeck for her help with the many nautical aspects of this book. A-D-2-8!

Chris Belsito for his ongoing support and public relations know-how.

A final thanks to members of "The Book Club" – Amy Reich, Dr. Robyn Lewis-Palmer, Andrea Wacker, and Patricia Gelmych – for their support and patience with the earlier versions of Second Wave.

As always, none of this would be possible without Connie and Murray Elder. Love you both dearly.

About the Author

Dr. Graham Elder was born in Montreal and attended McGill University for thirteen years, completing degrees in Physiotherapy, Medicine, and Orthopaedic Surgery. He now lives with his wife and two children (when they are not at university) in the small town of Sault Ste. Marie in Northern Ontario, cresting the shorelines of beautiful Lake Superior, where he runs a busy surgical and academic practice with writing time divided between scientific publications and novels.

Second Wave came into being as a result of excessive downtime from repeated COVID-19 lockdowns and is, once again, the consequence of an overactive imagination somewhat constrained by the realities of science …

Learn more about the author at:

https://twodocswriting.com

https://grahamelder.com

BOOKS IN THIS SERIES:

A COVID ODYSSEY

Snapshots in time of the Covid-19 pandemic as told through the escapism adventures of ER physician, Dr. Mark Spencer.

Series featured as part of the Pandemic Collection in the Museum of Health Care at Kingston. Written during the pandemic, about the pandemic.

Book 1 – A Covid Odyssey

A race against time to bring the cure for a deadly virus to a dying spouse.

Although the COVID-19 pandemic is ravaging the world, Dr. Mark Spencer's small town in Northern Ontario is largely unaffected other than being in lockdown and preparing for the potential onslaught. When his wife, Sarah – already attending a conference in Florida when the borders close – becomes deathly ill, she is admitted to a local hospital with minimal resources to treat Covid patients. As she spirals downward and with time running out, Mark concocts a plan to bring her an experimental anti-viral drug that might save her life. He must first, however, cross the Ontario/Michigan border and then travel 2000 km through a pandemic American landscape. Along his journey, he encounters a variety of unusual characters that bring into question the very foundation of his scientific beliefs.

Will Mark arrive at the hospital in time to save his wife?

No matter what, Mark's life will be forever changed by his Covid Odyssey.

Book 2 - Second Wave

A physician's harrowing intercontinental journey to uncover a dying father's potential cure for Covid-19.

Dr. Mark Spencer's life has finally returned to some degree of pandemic normalcy when he receives a heart-breaking phone call from his mother, who lives in England. His estranged father, a well-known virologist, has Covid and is being admitted to hospital. That same day, a letter arrives in the mailbox claiming that his father has discovered a cure for Covid-19, but that, for reasons unclear, Mark must go to England to retrieve it. Deciding that the possibility of a cure outweighs all else, Mark embarks on a gut-wrenching transatlantic trek that will ultimately push his resilience to the very limit.

Will Mark's treacherous voyage deliver him in time to uncover his father's secrets?

Join Dr. Spencer as he once again tackles the pandemic landscape in A Covid Odyssey – Second Wave.

Book 3 - Variant Reset

How far would a father go to save his dying daughter?

Alpha, Beta, Gamma, Delta . . . Omicron . . . Greek letters that have plummeted our world into chaos and tragedy.

Dr. Mark and Sarah Spencer are the proud parents of baby June, now four months old, born during the pandemic. The deadly Delta wave is waning, but there is a new variant on the horizon, the ferociously contagious Omicron that has a mortal predilection for infants. Somehow, despite every conceivable precaution, June has it and is quickly spiralling downhill.

Thanks to his father's research, Mark has spent the last year developing a drug that could cure not only Covid but all viral diseases, potentially changing a world on the verge of lockdown implosion. His team is close, so close, however, the well of their special ingredient has run dry, thanks to supply chain disruption. But an alternate source has been found in Central America at a location known only by one man.

Mark embarks on a transcontinental journey to beat the clock and save his daughter. There's a catch: A billion-dollar industry, Big Pharma, that wants to stop him. Using every conceivable manner of transportation,

Mark and his two friends will risk everything to save his daughter.

Wouldn't you?

Join Dr. Spencer as he struggles through the pandemic landscape for a third time in A Covid Odyssey – Variant Reset.

Book 4 - End In Sight

Death is not always the end …

While hiking the deep woods of Lake Superior Park in Northern Ontario, an innocent man is shot and killed. Somehow straddling the world of the living and the dead, he realizes he has until sunset to make peace with the loss of his loved ones and make sense of the reasons behind his death.

A reluctant killer.
A small-town deputy chief on the hunt for a murderer.
A wife who would do anything to protect her husband.
A niece on the verge of a monumental scientific discovery.
A physician on a mercy mission.

Five individuals whose paths cross over the course of a single day, changing their lives forever.

Follow Dr. Mark Spencer on a magical journey between worlds as he unravels the mystery and discovers something that could change the course of the pandemic.